KNOW BY HEART

Cole's hand reached for Jesse's hair, tapering at the back of her neck. Her arms wrapped around his back as his lips came down to hers. They both turned sideways as their bodies joined.

The touch of his lips on her sent Jesse ablaze. The kiss was demanding and hungry and her body's response was immediate. She kissed him back, digging her fingers into his back.

Cole felt an animal hunger start in his groin and spread throughout his body. His hand gently held her head, while the other went to her waist. The material of her dress could not contain the heat he felt from her body. His lips pressed against hers, wanting more. His breathing was out of control. He heard a moan escape Jesse, and his tongue entered her mouth. This time the moan was his as the taste of her was sweet and warm, throwing his world out of order.

BOOK YOUR PLACE ON OUR WEBSITE AND MAKE THE ARABESQUE ROMANCE CONNECTION!

We've created a customized website just for our very special Arabesque readers, where you can get the inside scoop on everything that's going on with Arabesque romance novels.

When you come online, you'll have the exciting opportunity to:

- View covers of upcoming books

- Learn about our future publishing schedule (listed by publication month and author)

- Find out when your favorite authors will be visiting a city near you

- Search for and order backlist books

- Check out author bios and background information

- Send e-mail to your favorite authors

- Join us in weekly chats with authors, readers and other guests

- Get writing guidelines

- AND MUCH MORE!

Visit our website at
http://www.arabesquebooks.com

KNOW BY HEART

Angela Winters

ARABESQUE

BET
BOOKS

BET Publications, LLC
www.bet.com
www.arabesquebooks.com

This book is dedicated to my little love, Jordan. I promise to miss you every day.

AUTHOR'S NOTE

Know By Heart is a fictional story set in "Silicon Valley" in California. This is not a town, valley, or city. This is a name given to a stretch of approximately thirty miles along the bay at the southern tip of San Francisco from Palo Alto to San Jose. Approximately twenty cities touch the valley, from Mountain View to San Mateo to Menlo Park. It is a densely packed area within Santa Clara County with approximately two million people. The term "Silicon Valley" was coined because of the many high-tech firms in the area that design devices made from high-purity silicon.

Chapter One

The crowd was chanting in protest louder now, the loudest since they'd started an hour ago.

"Silicon Valley for everyone!"

"End racism in Silicon Valley!"

"Full disclosure Top Pressure!"

"Silicon Valley for everyone!"

Jesse Grant had to take a deep breath. Finally, she thought. They were stopping now that they had reached their destination. She knew it had been a while since she'd exercised regularly, but following the crowd up the steep San Jose hill had winded her.

"Note to self," she whispered as she turned on her minirecorder. "Put jogging back on the daily schedule."

She lowered the recorder, her mind wandering to the

place where it somehow found itself every day. To the beach, where she used to jog. To him.

Peter Jackson, a local activist, raised his poster in the air. He wasn't chanting for the moment, so Jesse took the opportunity to do her job. She lifted the recorder.

"Now, Peter," she said. "You've led this crowd of protestors through downtown San Jose to Top Pressure's offices. Now that you've reached your destination, what do you want?"

He leaned forward, his raisin brown skin wrinkling early because of life under the California sun. "We want Top Pressure to know they aren't getting away with anything. The facts are, this company is a major sports software corporation now, employing almost one thousand people. Of those, only two are minorities, neither of whom is in an executive position."

"How do you know this, Peter?" Not a stranger to activism herself, Jesse could see the conviction in his eyes and she immediately liked him. He was one of the good guys, one that believed in equality and justice because it was right, not because it brought the cameras and tape recorders out.

"We had to force our way in to find out," he answered. "You see, when a recent report on the status of minorities in high tech solicited employment data, Top Pressure refused to comply. When the data was requested, they were a privately owned company. However, since then, they have become a publicly traded company and owe the public that information."

"And they have not complied?"

"No," Peter continued. "They kept stalling. Until the good people of Silicon Valley pressured the government to let us in and find out for ourselves. Suddenly the numbers appear. Not to our surprise, we find two minority employees out of almost a thousand. We suggested a civilized conversation about the issues. The response we received was a mere form letter saying Top Pressure is an equal opportunity employer. But their hiring practices don't fit with that statement."

"So this protest was the next step?" Jesse knew as a reporter she had to be as objective as possible. But she couldn't help but be angry with Top Pressure.

"After a couple more unanswered requests for a sit-down with the community."

Cole Nicholson heard the protestors shouting as soon as he turned the corner. He saw the crowd gathered across the street, disrupting traffic. What was the problem this time? He clutched the bag holding his Chinese takeout in his hand as he reached the steps to his office building.

"Looks like Top Pressure has some problems, Mr. Nicholson."

Cole nodded to James Midkif, a summer intern who delivered the mail to his office every day. Being a software company, Top Pressure was a competitor. Video games was a big business, and fiercely dog-eat-dog. Cole knew he should be interested in whatever trouble they might be having, but he wasn't. He wasn't interested in much of anything but work right now . . . work he had to get back to.

Then he saw her. Why she caught his eye among the several dozen people around he wasn't sure. No, that wasn't true. He was sure. She was incredibly beautiful, and that was why he spotted her now as he had that day on the beach months ago. Yes, it was her. The woman who'd broken his concentration as he jogged on the beach. Right where the chipped red wood bench sat. No one had been able to distract him from his jogging zone-out in the five years he had been jogging that same stretch of beach every weekday morning. Not even the women that jogged in bikinis that were a size or two too small. But her, this one who'd just popped up one morning about three months ago, had caught his eye and never let go. The sun had somehow shone brighter on her, and he'd been hooked on that very first day. She had been like a breeze when she jogged by. Time had slowed in a world where a thirty-hour day still wasn't enough. They had never spoken, only exchanged loaded glances and respectfully flirtatious smiles as they passed each other. Seeing her every morning had become the highlight of his day. Then, as abruptly as she'd appeared, a month ago she'd stopped coming. Cole's life had been thrown out of whack for a while after not seeing her. He hadn't forgotten her, couldn't have even if he tried. And now, here she was again. It seemed like years since he'd seen her. He was beginning to wonder if she had even been real, or some hallucination he had created to convince himself he still had a life despite this work madness of the past few months. But she was real, and as soon as he'd gotten over the shock of seeing her, his mind formed the question: Why had she stopped coming to the beach?

So, she was a reporter, he assumed from the scene before him. She was interviewing the man who appeared to be the ringleader of the event. Her familiar glowing chocolate brown skin, generous dark eyes, seductive lips that would scare any man, a healthy figure that was flattered by a sundress that let her curves determine its fit. He liked this much better than the oversized T-shirt and biking shorts she jogged in every day, although she even managed to make that look good. He loved her wavy black hair cut short to her head, as if her face didn't want the competition and didn't need the hassle. It didn't matter. Her face, which he had come to know every inch of, couldn't be matched by even the most beautiful hair in the world. Especially not with that dimple on her left cheek when she smiled.

Maybe he could take a few minutes away from work. He'd passed up the chance to talk to her before and thought she was gone forever.

"This is the issue." Peter returned his attention to Jesse after leading the group in several chants. "You got over two million people in this valley and surrounding areas. This high-tech haven. Of which, twenty-seven percent are Hispanic, over four percent African American, and nineteen percent Asian. So you tell me, with the population fifty percent minority, how does a company of a thousand have only two minorities in it? No matter what your hiring practices are, if you're complying with the law in the least, the numbers should be higher."

"What do you want Top Pressure to do?" Jesse asked.

"Disclose their records!" A young Latina woman interjected, almost pushing her way to Jesse. "That's what we want. I've got three friends with high-tech jobs in the area that applied for positions here. Each one of them with an Ivy League MBA and at least five years of tech experience. None of them were hired. Even though the company claims to be begging for employees."

The woman's confession sparked a tempered discussion

between observers and protestors. Jesse realized there was a big story here and was glad Peter had called her.

It was hotter than usual this June morning, and Jesse reached in her backpack for her water bottle. Taking a sip, she glanced across the building crowd, across the street. That's when she saw him, and the bottle almost slipped out of her hand.

He was looking right at her; she could tell that much, even at this distance. The crowd around him faded a bit, as she felt a distinct pull to him. The same she felt every time she saw him and his dark chocolate brown skin, muscular build, hazel eyes, and broad nose. It was that same black, clean cut hair and flawlessly shaven face that she remembered more than she cared to admit. It was a shock to her, but she blinked and looked again, then saw him clearly standing taller than any of the men around him.

Many times, she wondered if she would ever see him again after she had stopped jogging on the beach. Hoping she would, hoping she wouldn't. Now she was looking right at him, and the feelings it stirred in her, she knew by heart. Instead of the Stanford University T-shirt and baggy shorts she'd seen him jog in almost every day for a month, today he was dressed like most of the men in Silicon Valley: like he had money, but worked so much that he never took the time to actually shop for high-priced clothes. His wardrobe was casual, probably whatever he could order off the Internet. She imagined he did everything off the Internet, as most people in Silicon Valley did.

Still, Jesse had to admit it worked for him. He was attractive, very attractive. And that was why . . . she didn't want to think about it anymore. The thoughts of their early morning encounters, the smiles and occasional nods, made her want to walk over to him, but she fought it. She fought it because she wanted to so badly. He made her think of her past, the past she was trying to get away from. She had to remind herself of that to make herself turn away from him. It was just too dangerous.

But then he smiled. He smiled that smile that she had found herself looking forward to every weekday morning. And just as before, Jesse felt her knees go weak. She smiled back because she couldn't do anything else.

"Smoke and mirrors," Peter Jackson said. "Smoke and mirrors is all it was a few years ago when everyone kept talking about minorities in high tech. Yeah, yeah, yeah. It's a bad thing, we'll do something about it. So what's happened? Nothing really. A few companies have changed things around. But others, those like Top Pressure, are still saying they'll do something about it. Well, now we'll do something about it."

Her smile sent a surge of energy through Cole. He knew he had to . . .

"Cole! Cole, there you are."

Cole turned to see Debra Kennedy, the assistant to the CEO of his company, coming toward him.

"Chris is looking for you," she said, her fire-engine red hair frizzing in the humidity. She repositioned her librarian-style glasses. "He says it's urgent."

"What is it?" Cole asked as she passed him.

Debra didn't stop, only turning her head over her shoulder as she kept on. "No telling with him. Just hurry. He's calling all over for you. He's ticked you turned your cell phone off."

Cole grabbed his phone out of his back pocket. "Damn battery."

He looked up at the woman again, gripping the lunch in his hand. She had turned away, disappointing him terribly. He wanted to . . . needed to . . . but he couldn't. Maybe her turning away was for the best.

A woman was the last thing he needed to concern himself with, even though she was no ordinary woman. There was too much to get done. Besides, he had made a promise to himself, to his product and his future. That was why he wouldn't approach her now, why he hadn't approached her any of those days on the beach. And, oh yeah, there was Tracy . . . and she was one woman who would not be forgotten. Cole knew he had avoided that issue for too long.

No. He had no time for this woman, even though he wanted desperately to speak to her. So, with one last look at the young beauty who had a permanent place in his mind, Cole turned and headed into the building. Back to work.

Jesse nodded at Peter, letting him know she understood what he was saying. But as much as she cared about the issue and tried to stay with him on it, she was distracted, and eventually her attention forced her to turn back to him, back across the street.

He was gone. She felt her shoulders lower in defeat, hoping he would stay interested, but almost glad that he hadn't. After all, what would she have done? Walked over to him? What if he had walked over to her? She would have done the same thing she had all those other days she had seen him and wanted to approach him. Nothing. Not after what she'd just been through. There was no room in her life for a man. Back to work.

* * *

"Another painting of a naked man?"

Jesse asked the question as she stood behind her best friend, Joan Griffin.

"It's my vision." Joan tilted her head back and rolled her eyes at Jesse. She put her brush down and assessed the painting. "Don't make fun of my masterpieces. I don't make fun of yours."

"I'm not making fun of it," Jesse said, placing her hands on Joan's shoulders. "It's just that we've been taking this art class once a week for two months now, and every one of your free paintings is a naked man."

"I don't know what you're talking about." Joan whisked an imaginary bug out of her face, the air moving a few strands of her thinly braided fine hair.

"I'm talking about whether it's a bowl of fruit or a vase on the stand, you paint a naked man. Today, for example, the teacher placed an arrangement of lilies in the middle of the room."

"I painted a bed of lilies," Joan said defiantly.

"With a naked brother lying on them." Jesse tapped the back of Joan's head. The girl had issues. That was why she liked her so much.

"You've got a problem with naked men?" Joan asked.

Jesse smiled, her white teeth shining between full lips. "Paint on, sister."

"Besides," Joan mumbled, "you're only a layer of cotton away from me."

Jesse shrugged as she looked at her own painting. "This is a sidewalk scene."

Joan pointed at the painting on the easel right next to her own. "Please, girl. All this scenery is backdrop. That brother on the steps of that building is the subject of your painting. You aren't fooling anybody."

Jesse blushed. She looked around the empty classroom to make sure no one heard. No, everyone had left. Joan always lagged behind, making her late.

Jesse was too embarrassed to tell Joan that she couldn't think of anything but that man, The Jogger, the name she had given him the first day she'd seen him. The name she had whispered in her sleep.

"Hey." Joan leaned sideways, looking closer at the picture. Her brows furrowed. "You've drawn him before haven't you? I could swear . . ."

"Don't be ridiculous." Jesse quickly covered the painting with the satin flip wrap. She had painted him before, painted him jogging. But how could she explain that? Joan would have a field day with that, already being one to overanalyze everything. "He's nothing more than a stick figure. All the people I draw look the same."

"Touchy, touchy." Joan gave her a once-over. "If I didn't know you better, I'd say I just struck a nerve. You are way too attached to your art. No one is going to pass judgment on you."

Jesse pretended to laugh. Although she loved the art class she'd suggested to Joan they take on the campus of San Jose State University, she was tired. It had been a long day, and she was hoping a good night's sleep could get The Jogger off her mind. She was still reeling from seeing him again.

She looked at herself in the mirror next to the door of the classroom though. She had paint on her cheek and her leg. Despite her smock, her jean overall shorts had paint on them, too. She couldn't be neat if she staked her life on it. It wasn't just her clothes though. Her eyes also told of her long day.

"Quit staring at yourself in the mirror, girl." Joan had twirled her seat around, watching her. "Everybody knows you're cute."

Jesse laughed. "Thanks, but I know I look a mess."

Joan rolled her eyes. "I should be so lucky to look a mess like you."

Joan sold herself short. Jesse had told her that more times than she could count. She was a beautiful twenty-five-year-old black woman. She was tall, thin, with a good heart and cynical sense of humor that made you laugh at things you knew you shouldn't. She'd taken Jesse under her wing the second she had moved to San Jose, and had been there for her since. Jesse hadn't been the easiest person to get along with while dealing with what she had just escaped.

Jesse grabbed her purse. "Let's skip the ice cream run. I gotta get out of here, girl. Us old gals need to get some rest."

Joan shrugged. "Yeah, right. What are you, twenty-eight? Careful where you step, old gal. Don't want to break a hip or anything."

"How long you plan on staying here?" Jesse asked. "I don't want you out late by yourself."

"Are you on your fear trip again?" Joan's eyes softened. "He's not here, Jesse. He's in prison in Chicago."

Jesse sighed. "This is not about Henry, Joan. Despite what people think, there are actual crimes committed on Silicon Valley streets."

Joan feigned fear, mocking with quivering hands. "Ohhh! Alone at night in Silicon Valley. What's going to happen? Maybe some teenagers will drive by and hurl insults at me like 'Your mother's computer only has a 12X CD-Rom.'"

Jesse waved a dismissing hand at her. "That's the last I worry about you. Just watch out. I'll see you tomorrow at work."

"Unless I win the lotto." Joan returned to her painting.

Jesse stepped outside the campus building. She didn't keep walking, instead stopping out of habit. It was a normal beautiful night in San Jose, but it wasn't the weather that stopped her. It was her memories. Memories of not being able to step outside alone night or day because of her ex-boyfriend, Henry. She had escaped to San Jose and had been here for almost six months, but still she expected to see him. Less often than six months ago, but still.

Tonight, all Jesse saw was Sabrina Joseph standing at the bus stop near the parking lot. Sabrina was in her art class. She kept to herself mostly, but was polite. She was a full-figured woman, caramel colored, in her mid-thirties. She had short hair, cut to her head like Jesse's, the color a vibrant light brown, almost dirty blond.

Jesse liked what little she knew of her. She had always liked the off-center types, considering herself one of them. Sabrina wasn't a conformist. She dressed in a hippie-meets-Southwest style, wore no makeup, and all her paintings were abstract. She was a little disorganized, a lot klutzy.

"Sabrina?" Jesse stopped as she approached. "Waiting for the bus?"

"Yeah." She always had that apologetic look on her face, like she was inconveniencing you by making you listen to her. "My usual ride can't pick me up. I think it should be here in twenty minutes or so. I hope I got the time right."

"Let me give you a ride. It's not well lit over here, and it's almost ten."

"No, no." She reached for a folder that had dropped. "I couldn't."

"Where do you live?" Jesse grabbed a notebook that was close to falling out of Sabrina's oversized, overstuffed bag.

"Right on the edge of San Jose. Near Burbank."

"Fine." Jesse was already headed for the car. "You're right near me. Let's go."

Getting anywhere with Sabrina wasn't simple, Jesse soon found out. The woman had a couple of bags, none of them the right size for anything she needed to carry. With every three or four steps, the two women had to stop to pick up a folder, a writing pad, or a pen Sabrina had dropped. Not to mention the flimsy purse Sabrina had that couldn't seem to stay on her shoulder.

"Are you all right?" Jesse asked, noticing that Sabrina couldn't sit still in the passenger seat.

Sabrina let out a sharp, sarcastic laugh. "I'm alive. That's all I can say on the positive side right now."

"That can't be entirely true. What's wrong?"

"What isn't is probably the better question. Trust me, you don't want to hear any of my numerous sob stories. I'd probably break down and cry on you. Then what would you do?"

"I wouldn't mind," Jesse said. "Crying is good for the soul. It's cleansing."

"If that's the case, I should be squeaky-clean by now."

Sabrina adjusted the bag on her lap so she could lean against the side window. However, the move neglected her sack purse, which spilled out onto the floor mat. With a frustrated curse, she reached down to retrieve it.

"Sorry for cursing," she said after a while.

"That can be cleansing sometimes, too." Jesse reached over and gave Sabrina a comforting pat.

"Thanks," Sabrina managed a half smile.

The night breeze cooled them through the car windows. The only words spoken for a while were Sabrina's driving directions. The view was a valid distraction from conversation. San Jose was an attractive city at night.

San Jose was a big city, too. Given the title "The Capital of the Silicon Valley," it was California's third largest city, and the eleventh largest city in the U.S. It was the center of a densely packed area of towns, such as Mountain View and Palo Alto, where the famous Stanford University stood. Its streets were lined with modern buildings and overpriced homes. The mixture of modern architecture and nineteenth-century Victorians and mission-style buildings gave the city a unique character. The different lighting styles made for beautiful scenery against the darkness.

"Are you sure you don't want to talk about it?" Jesse asked after Sabrina's third heavy sigh in a row.

"You and Joan are lucky," she said, as if ignoring the question. "Your friendship. It seems strong."

Jesse smiled, making a hard left. "I love that crazy girl. We work together at the Silicon Valley Weekly. When I moved here, she took me under her wing and showed me the city, introduced me to friends. She made me feel like she had known me for years. We really clicked."

"You're a newbie? How long have you been here?" Sabrina twisted in her seat to face Jesse.

"Six months. The way people are moving out here for the jobs, I guess six months makes me a veteran. I moved here from Chicago." She paused, thinking of a reason she could tell that was other than the truth. "For the job at the paper. Joan lives down the street from me. She's been great, filling me in on the Silicon Valley lingo and lifestyle."

"You live here six months and already have a cute little best friend." Sabrina made a smacking sound with her tongue. "I've lived here ten years and have yet to . . . "

"Come on, Sabrina. You can't say in ten years you haven't found a friend."

The tears came immediately, surprising Jesse. She wasn't sure how to respond.

Sabrina spoke through sobs. "I thought . . . I thought . . ."

Jesse wondered what she had started. "Sabrina, I . . ."

"She was supposed to be my friend," she went on, "but I was so stupid. I'm not the outgoing, free-spirited type like you. I don't attract people to me in droves. I know people, but . . . she was my only real friend. Or so I thought. I trusted her with . . ."

Jesse wondered if she should pull over. She kept glancing from Sabrina to the road.

"She stole my fiancé from me." The words tumbled out as Sabrina's hands clenched into fists. "I was supposed to be married last Saturday. Been planning it for a year. Lost my friend, my lover. He was the only man that treated me worth anything. She knew that, how much he meant to me. I just can't . . ."

Jesse placed a free arm on her shoulder, her memories of trust betrayed creating sincere sympathy. "Love and trust can be a cold hard lesson, but it's one that we all learn. It seems like the end of the world, and it sort of is for a while."

"Turn left here," Sabrina managed through sniffles. "I'm at the end of this block."

"You're good with directions," Jesse said, as if it would make a difference. She pulled up to the rare two flat. The porch light showed sun-faded blue and dirty white sidings and windows. It was old, probably more worn down than the night told.

"I'm so sorry to fall apart like this." Sabrina fumbled around for her folders and bags. "It's just been so hard on me lately. Sometimes I feel like I'm drowning."

"I understand, Sabrina." Jesse knew exactly what the older woman meant. She, too, felt things very deeply. Her heart had been broken more than enough times, and pain was unmerciful. "Be strong, sister. The tide always turns."

Sabrina opened the door halfway. Another sigh. "How old are you, twenty-five?"

"Twenty-eight." Jesse always wondered why so many women focused on age, as if the two numbers defined your life, your options. Did it even matter if she was twenty-eight? She felt from sixteen to one hundred years old on any given day.

"You don't look a day over twenty-five," she said. "Well, I'm thirty-five. With the very few eligible black men in the valley, I don't stand a chance against cute little things like you."

"Now, Sabrina. It's not about that." Jesse hated the way black women saw each other as different degrees of competition. "You won't have to compete with anyone for the man that's right for you."

"That's what I thought." She shrugged, apparently not convinced. "Good night, Jesse. Thanks for the ride."

"See you next Thursday night?"

Sabrina shrugged again. "I don't know. I haven't been feeling very artistic lately."

Jesse watched until Sabrina was safely inside, after recovering dropped folders and runaway purse straps at least five times, before driving off.

Jesse reflected on Sabrina's somber words. It was definitely slim pickings in Silicon Valley, where single black men were as scarce as snow shovels. Joan had found one in Ray Stone. Two years and going strong. She was holding on tight, too. Joan was more of a realist than a romantic like Jesse. She had a good black man, and was never willing to risk him by pretending that it was as simple as love. She wasn't taking any chances. Any attempt by another woman to get Ray's attention, and it was on.

Jesse felt for women like Sabrina. It wasn't easy. She knew it was hard to be alone when that wasn't what you wanted. She considered herself a woman secure in her sexuality, comfortable with her own desires and in love with being in love. Aware of the emotional—not to mention physical—needs a man could fulfill, she was always happy to be in a relationship. Especially if the guy didn't try to domesticate her.

Right now, however, finding a man wasn't an issue for Jesse. After what she'd just been through, what she'd had to come out to California to get away from, a man was the last thing she needed.

Except him. Thoughts of her beach jogger standing on those steps brought that familiar feeling only he seemed to be able to bring. A part of her felt like such a fool for not going after him when the interview was over. But it was that part of her that had almost gotten her killed a little over six months ago. She was almost angry at herself for thinking of him so much. She knew all she needed was a good night's sleep.

"No," she said to herself, turning the radio on and cranking it loud to drown out her thoughts. "No men. Not even him."

* * *

"We've got problems. Big problems."

Cole Nicholson's head jolted up from his laptop as he was snapped from his thoughts. Problems. He didn't need any more problems. He was already mad at himself for thinking too much of her and whether or not he had made the biggest mistake of his life by not approaching her. After all, what were the odds that he'd come across her again? Silicon Valley wasn't a small area. But still, there she was.

His hazel eyes blinked as he tried to focus on Chris. It was almost ten P.M. He'd thought he was alone at the office.

"Don't tell me I scared you, Cole." Chris Spall strode with his usual mastery into Cole's corner office and placed himself in the leather chair on the other side of the desk. "I thought nothing scared you."

Cole laughed, his confidence showing a hint of appreciation for his boss's compliment. Only a hint. If he'd learned anything as a black man in corporate America, it was that showing too much appreciation cost you respect, which was already too hard to earn in tech heaven.

"You thought right," he said, leaning back. His trim, muscled arms stretched out as he yawned and met again behind his head as his fingers entwined. He smiled naturally. "Never scared. I would say mildly surprised."

Chris laughed. He placed a sun-tanned hand on his chest, his fingers invading the space between the buttons of his sharply starched white shirt. Not a wrinkle in sight, even after a long workday. The fingers in his shirt was his thing, his gesture. Every man had one.

"As expected, Cole. You never surprise me. Never back down, never show a weakness. You treat business like war. That's why I like you."

"What's up, Chris?" Cole noticed the smile fade. Chris was obviously upset. "You said we have big problems."

"What are you doing here so late, Cole?" His blue eyes sparkled, contrasting with the gloomy look on his face.

"I was just about to ask you the same question." Cole noticed Chris's nervous gesture, a hand through his premature gray hair three times in a row at a very quick pace. "You're the one with a wife and kid."

"Well, I figure if you're working late, I better stick around for appearances. You'll have my job soon enough. I just want to make sure it's not too soon."

They understood each other. Cole appreciated that. When he'd joined Netstyles three years ago as director of business development, Chris had been looking for someone to groom, to take over the company he had created only two years earlier. He was planning to retire at the old age—according to Silicon Valley standards—of forty, but he wasn't going to leave his creation to just anyone. He'd had one of the best headhunters on the West Coast contact Cole and taken it from there.

Cole had taken his Ivy League degrees and technology industry experience and made the company a midsized player in the highly competitive Internet software game. The company joined the dotcom stock market on the shoulders of his designs. Cole made himself and a few others millionaires, and, more important, he made Chris a multimillionaire. Unlike seventy-five percent of the dotcoms that came out with a blast only to fizzle fast due to lack of funding and waning customer interest, Netstyles was a survivor, and a Wall Street darling.

Now, as the chief architect of Netstyles at thirty, Cole was primed to take over. That was, of course, after revealing his next blockbuster, which he had been devoting his entire life to for the past six months. After this product hit the market, even Chris's future grandkids would be set for life, and he would ride off into the sunset. Cole understood that patience was a virtue, and he savored every bit of the lessons Chris taught him. Still, he was excited about the future.

Chris's eyes wandered a second around the cherry-wood-and-black-marble decorated room before returning to Cole, his desk, and his computer.

"What is it, Chris?" Cole asked again.

"We knew we had to place some serious security on alert.com."

Cole sat up straight, his eyes widening. Alert.com was his baby, his product, his next big thing. It would be the Internet service that catapulted him into CEO world and took Netstyles from midsized to major player.

"What's happened?" Cole asked.

Chris shook his head, holding a hand up. "Don't panic yet."

Cole darted up from his seat, pacing the room. "We've taken all the proper precautions. We've limited the people involved, not released a word outside. Every single document is password protected and access checked hourly by the security system."

"I don't think it's us," Chris said with his head down. "I think it's the chip."

"Syndot?" Cole knew this would happen. "We never should've partnered with them!"

"What were we supposed to do? Make the chip ourselves? We're software, not hardware, Cole. We needed a
partner. Syndot had the best reputation for . . ."

"Just tell me what's going on." Cole wouldn't bring up
the fact that he should've managed the partnership. He
had been so tied up in developing the product, he'd agreed
to let Chris and the new business development director,
Paul Brown, oversee the relationship. He simply hadn't
had the time.

"Someone is investigating me." Chris's eyes blinked rapidly, nervously. "Someone is checking up on me, and they
seem to want to relate it to Syndot."

Cole stuffed anxious hands in the pockets of his khakis.
"Why would anyone want to . . . how do you know?"

"I sent Debra for the documents. You know, since we're
pretty much done with Syndot."

Cole felt his temper heating up. "Debra is *not* on our
need-to-know list. She has no contract of secrecy with us
for this product. Why was she sent?"

"Can we not deal with the side stuff now?" Chris sighed
impatiently. "She's my admin, for Pete's sake, and she did
sign the proprietary information noncompete like everyone else here. The deal with Syndot is complete anyway.
The contract for percentages is set in stone, so all the
remaining correspondences needed to be shredded."

"They couldn't do that themselves?" One million give-
and-takes flashed in Cole's mind. There wasn't a lot he
wouldn't do to protect his product.

"You're the one who said we can't trust them for that.
You wanted the notarized sheets back here, so we could
shred them. I said . . ."

"Chris . . ." Cole's eye was squinting impatiently. He

walked a fine line with Chris at times. Sometimes he got irritated with his nervous babbling and the roles reversed. Chris seemed to accept it since Cole was usually in the right, and he never pushed it too far.

"Some documents were missing." Chris leaned forward in the chair, appearing exhausted. "Those idiots. Brad— you know, our guy—said he gathered every damn document we shared and put them in a folder ready for us 'cause he thought Debra was coming yesterday."

Cole knew what was next. "Don't tell me he left the folder out instead of under lock and key as our agreements instructed."

"He said the day got crazy. By the end of it, the folder was lost under a pile of papers."

Cole leaned over the desk, placing his hands down flat and firmly. "He left them out all night? When did he figure it out?'

"When Debra showed up today to pick them up. That was about ten in the morning."

Cole threw his hands in the air.

"Don't panic yet," Chris said. "We did what we had to do. Found out there was a temporary in the office. A temp in the cleaning crew."

"Why didn't you tell me before now?"

Chris's voice lowered. "I didn't need an ugly scene that early in the day."

"What do we have on this temp?" Cole didn't need to contemplate if there was a connection. That temp stole the papers.

"Security cameras have her picture, we interviewed the other cleaners." Chris shook his head. "Somehow she was a replacement for a Trina Lopez, who was sick. None of them seem to know who she was. The name she gave was fake. We'll find her. We know what she looks like and have some other clues."

"Which papers did she get?" Cole tried to calm down.

"Some merger notes. A few chip details and estimation rollout dates."

Cole noticed the look of despair. "You still have your copies, right?"

Chris nodded.

"Let's pull them and see exactly what she has. Where are the rest of the papers?"

"Debra got them."

Cole nodded, breathing at a regular pace again. His mind was already going, figuring out what to do. "What's the motive?"

"Does it matter?" Chris asked.

"It might tell us what she plans to do with the information."

"My maid said there was a woman loitering around the house a week ago. She fits the same description. I've gotten three calls from former business partners or friends of mine saying they've been contacted about me by a woman identifying herself as a detective or concerned family friend."

"A detective?"

"Yeah, but the name she gave doesn't exist in any local department. She's trying to dig up dirt on me."

"About what?" Cole knew Chris well enough to assess that the man didn't have anything that dirty.

Chris shrugged. "Hell if I know. Cole, when we get more information on her . . . can I count on you to take care of this?"

Their eyes caught and locked in friendship and understanding, speaking the agreement of a commitment to keep control of a situation that could easily get out of control. Cole didn't have time to check for any hint of misunderstanding in Chris' eyes. He didn't have time to wonder why Chris seemed more intense than usual. There was no room for that now.

Cole nodded. "I'll fix everything, Chris. This won't slip out of our hands."

"I have some notes on what we have on the woman so far in my office."

"Good. Give me what you've got and we need to get Brad on the phone, too. I'll take care of the problem."

"We have to be willing to do anything, Cole."

Cole saw a glint of fire in Chris's eyes that was unusual for him. Not a good fire, a dangerous one.

"Anything," Chris repeated before slowly turning and heading out.

Cole gritted his teeth. For three years, he'd given his life to this company, to this product. He'd given up everything else for this. Who would steal his thunder?

"No one," he said to himself, as he reached for the phone.

"This better be good," the husky voice on the other end said. "My show is on."

"Dean, it's Cole."

"Cole! My boy. The dead awaken."

"It's been a while, I know." Cole knew everything had been a while, and in some sense he had been socially dead. "This is serious. We can catch up later."

"I've heard that before."

"I've got a job for you. I need you to pull out your magic hat."

"You know I'm on probation, man. I can't hack anymore. I'm not even supposed to be near a computer for two more years."

"So what have you been doing to pay for the mortgage on that Mountain View condo?"

"Hit me, bro."

Chapter Two

Jesse pulled her car over to the side of the road to answer her cell phone. She glanced down at her watch. She was already late. It had to be work. No one else had the number.

"Jesse Grant here."

"Ha! Made you do it!"

"Joan!" Jesse gritted her teeth. "I'm going to strangle you. It's bad enough I have to have this cell phone. You know how much I despise those people who walk around, in-line skating, biking, jogging, and especially driving while talking on these ridiculous things. Why are you trying to turn me into one of them?"

Despite that, at Silicon Valley Weekly all reporters had a cell phone. House rules. Jesse tried never to use hers. Joan knew she hated it, which was why she teased her by calling her all the time.

Joan laughed while she spoke. "You're so easy. Where are you anyway?"

"I was on my way to work, but now I'm wasting time on the side of the road talking to you."

"You know the boss hates late lucys. Unless you're on a hot story."

"No such luck, but I am going to be later than usual today. I've got to drop by Sabrina Joseph's."

"Sabrina from art class? Why?"

"I gave her a ride home Thursday night after class. She had a bunch of folders with her."

"Dropping and falling all over the place, no doubt."

Jesse laughed. "You know her. She left one of them here. It slipped down the side of the passenger seat."

"You just now getting to that? It's Monday."

"I didn't spot it until this morning. I just happened to reach over there to get my sunglasses when they fell. I keep losing them when I make hard turns. They slide around and fall . . ."

"Yeah, that's very interesting," Joan interrupted. "Save the sunglasses story for the weekend. The folder. What does it say?"

"Girl, I'm not trying to be up in her business." Joan was so nosy, and it could get contagious. "I'm just gonna drop it off."

"Just take a look at it, woman. You're a journalist, for goodness sake. Where is your curiosity?"

Jesse's fingers trailed the closed folder. "Joan. She's not a story. She's a friend."

"Everything is a story, and she's not really a close friend. What could it be? You know it's always the quiet nobodies who lead the most interesting lives." Her tone was teasing.

"It's eating at you now. Tearing you apart. You must know . . ."

"You make me sick." Jesse reached for the folder. "And I'm telling Luke that you're spending his paper's money on frivolous cell phone calls."

"That old man loves me. Just give me the juice."

Jesse held the phone between her head and shoulder as her hands reached into the folder.

" 'Netstyles Corporation' is on the top of the page," she said while reading. "It's a software company right here in San Jose. It says the target is Chris Spall."

"She's a hit woman?"

"I sincerely doubt that," Jesse smirked. "I'm sure 'target' is referring to something else. There's something about hardware chips, alert.com, whatever that is. There are some rollout and contract compliances. Her writing is terrible. I can hardly read any of it. I think this says . . . yeah, I think she is suspicious of lies, theft, cover-up."

"Sounds good. What about lies, theft, and cover-up?"

"I can't say for sure. I don't know. I can't read it well at all." Jesse's curiosity was piqued. "It doesn't make sense. Like something is missing here. Wait, she's got a diary, too. Not the personal kind, but like a time tracker."

"About Chris Paul?"

"Spall. Yes, and the name Cole Nicholson keeps popping up next to his. Sound familiar?"

"No. Maybe they work at that company. What is the theft and cover-up about? What else does the diary say?"

"No, Joan." Jesse stuffed the papers back into the folder. "This is wrong. I listened to the woman's sob story the other night. She's really going through some bad stuff, and she trusted me enough to tell me about it. She just had the only friend she thought was real betray her. I'm not going to turn around and invade her privacy like this. She deserves better."

"Loser."

"Stop it, Joan."

"You're weak. You're soft."

"Good-bye!" Jesse hung up, checked the lane, and got back into traffic. She didn't need the ribbing, even if it was in jest. Traffic was hectic enough. Even with the trains and trolleys running regularly, Silicon Valley folks were drivers.

Journalism. This new career of hers. Joan was a die-hard paper junkie. She'd been a journalist since her junior high years, working on the school paper. She thought anything was free game. Jesse had a curious nature, a desire for the truth, and a commitment to helping her people. She'd always worked for charities and cause organizations, using her writing skills among others. So journalism wasn't that difficult a transition. But she wasn't sure if she had the stomach to invade other people's privacy to get a story. For the sake of the truth, maybe, but not for the sake of a story.

Especially after what had happened to her in Chicago. Her privacy had been practically ripped from her, sending her spiraling into fear and uncertainty. Sometimes it still felt like yesterday. And to make things worse, her beach jogger, who had reappeared so abruptly in her life, the one she had hoped a good night's sleep would make her forget last week, was the first thing on her mind when she'd awakened this morning, as he had been every morning since she had seen him again.

The flashing red and blue lights of the squad car came clearly into view as Jesse turned the corner. She parked her car, watching curiously. Yes, the onlookers were all gathering on the sidewalk in front of Sabrina's house.

With alarm, Jesse hurtled out of the car, not even thinking of the folder. A mixture of anxiety and excitement washed over her. She made her way past neighbors and an officer with his back to her, up the stairs, and into the house without hesitation.

"Hey!" A tall, thin officer in the hallway yelled to her as Jesse stumbled in. "Stop it. Stop right there."

She halted. "Where's Sabrina?"

"You know the victim?" This officer was of medium build. Coming around the corner with authority, he gave Jesse a once-over. "What's your name?"

"Victim?" Sydney's eyes quickly scanned the country-style house. It wasn't ransacked. It was extremely neat. "Where is she?"

"Ma'am," the officer spoke calmly, but with a cold wrap around his tone. "I've asked you a question. What is your name?"

"Jesse Grant," she answered firmly, trying to calm herself. "I'm a friend of Sabrina's. We have a class together. I dropped her off Thursday night. What happened to her?"

"She's dead." An elderly Latina woman entered the hallway from behind the medium-build officer. She was short and petite, dressed in a paisley housedress. She looked drained of energy.

"I'm Grace, her neighbor. I found her."

"You were with her Thursday night?" the officer asked.

"Yes," Jesse answered. "Our art class is at San Jose State. I drove her home."

"What time did you last see her?"

Jesse shook her head. "A little after ten. What happened?"

"What was her mood?"

"I don't know." Jesse was getting irritated with all the questions and no answers. "She was upset. She had some bad things happen to her recently. Now I've answered quite a few of your questions. How about answering one or two of mine?"

The officer's expression showed his distaste for Jesse's questioning. She had no expectation of getting anything from him. She turned to Grace. "Do you know what happened?" she asked.

"I came to check on her," Grace said. "She's always in the garden by ten on Saturday and Sunday. Like clockwork. I come out, too, to tend mine. We always talk. Although lately, she hadn't been . . . well, as you said, she'd had some bad experiences. Last Sunday, she hadn't come out, so I checked in on her. She was very upset. She'd just heard her ex got engaged to someone. I think it was a friend of hers. She didn't want company. Monday is garbage day, but she didn't come out. So I came by."

"What brings you by this morning?" the officer asked Jesse.

"Tell me what happened," Jesse said, her eyes narrowed in his direction.

"Ms. Lopez here." He nodded to Grace. "She found her dead when she came to check on her. Ms. Joseph committed suicide. What looks like midnight last night."

"Suicide?" Jesse was in disbelief. "How do you know it was suicide?"

"That doctor over there said she hasn't been harmed," Grace said. "I overheard him. He thinks she took something. I guess it was all too much. *Pobresita.* Losing the fiancé to her best friend. Money problems, too, I think. You know her mama died a while back."

"No, I didn't." Jesse felt for Sabrina. She remembered their conversation from the other night. "I knew it had been hard on her, but . . . What did her letter say?"

"What letter?" the officer asked.

"There was a suicide note, right?"

The officer shook his head. "No, but that's not necessary. It's a clear case."

Jesse saw the apathy in the officer's eyes, and a sense of alarm hit her. He was giving up. He had no intention of entertaining the possibility of foul play. "So, that's it? The fact that there was no note is enough to leave doubt. Aren't you going to investigate?"

He looked annoyed at her. "This isn't a detective show. Nice little clues like detailed suicide notes don't show up in the real world. We're going to contact her friends and family. We'll look for anyone with motive, but look around yourself. This place is pristine. The TV, CD player, everything of any value is still here. No one broke in, no locks were tampered with, no windows left open. There are no signs of a struggle, no bruises, no sign of rape, nothing. I've seen this plenty of times. It looks like she took some pills and ended it. If we see anything to the contrary, we'll investigate."

"Fine." Jesse was doubtful, although his words made sense. The place was spotless. "Still, if someone wanted to, they could cover their own tracks and make it appear like anything but murder. Grace, you knew her better than I did. Can you think of anyone who would want to kill her?"

"I don't know who they are exactly, but I'm sure there

are plenty of folks that would probably feel a little better with her dead."

"Why?" Jesse couldn't think of Sabrina in those terms. She couldn't imagine her being someone that could incur a wrath that would lead to murder.

"She made a living out of making enemies," Grace said. "Don't you know what she did for a living? She was a private investigator."

"Sabrina Joseph?" Jesse couldn't fit the person with the profession.

"Surprised me, too, when I heard. She paid her bills by catching cheating husbands and folks faking injuries for lawsuits. She testified in court dozens of times. I'm sure there were a lot of people who had a grudge against her."

Jesse turned to the officer. "So there you have it. Suspects."

He squinted a skeptical eye. "No signs of alarm in the house. She would have been alarmed if someone she was spying on dropped by. She wouldn't have let them in."

"Maybe they got in without her knowing," Grace added.

The officer looked thoroughly frustrated now. "Look, lady. I gotta work here. Do you mind?"

"I do mind, but I've got to get to work myself." Jesse rolled her eyes at the officer before returning to Grace. "Grace, can we keep in touch? I'm curious about this, aren't you?"

Grace nodded as the two headed for the door. "Well, now that you bring it up, I am. I wasn't before. I was pretty sure she had killed herself. We still don't know if she did or not."

"No, we don't." Jesse knew it was the journalist in her that saw beyond the simplistic. Joan would be proud. "It's just that suicide is so . . . you know. I'm also curious to see if the cops do their job."

Grace winked as if she were in on a high-level secret. "I got ya."

She took the card Jesse held out for her. "I'll give you a call later today."

Cole took a deep breath as he started his daily jog. He had a sense of excitement and anticipation that he had not felt in a while. Since he'd seen her last. She seemed to be the only thing that could make him feel like this. Not even his work could give him the rush she did. He blasted the Walkman and kept his eyes open.

He approached the spot, the usual spot where they would come across each other, near the red bench with the ad for a metal detector to find treasures under the sand. It was a garish, mostly tacky bench, but had come to represent so much more to Cole.

He slowed down, hoping, wondering. This would be different, wouldn't it? After all, they had seen each other again Thursday after a month. Didn't that mean something? Surely she would come back. Cole looked around. There was no one. No one but him. He felt stupid for even being there, wondering how this even got here, this illusion of a relationship he had created in his mind.

Cole stopped jogging, looked around one last time, and started heading back. He had no time for this anyway. Her or the jogging.

"Dead?"

"Dead." Jesse played around with her computer mouse,

not concentrating on her work. It was hard to concentrate on anything. She had gotten back to work in time for a staff meeting and was finally able to explain that morning's ordeal to Joan.

Joan leaned even further into Jesse's cube, her mouth wide open. "I can't believe it. Sabrina Joseph, a P.I.? Suicide? It all sounds fishy to me."

"Me too." Jesse clicked on her favorite Silicon Valley real estate site. She wasn't into this right now, but had made a commitment to spend her lunch time today on her seemingly hopeless search for a house. "I got that vibe you're always telling me about. The one I need to give myself over to."

"You make it sound like a joke. It's not. It's journalist intuition, and has spurred famous journalists on to changing the world. What are you doing, anyway? Aren't we going into San Fran for lunch? I've got a taste for a San Francisco hot dog."

"It's the same dog as right here," Jesse said.

"It's different. I can't explain it, but . . ."

"You're on your own today. I told you I'm working the hunt at lunch." Jesse clicked on a house she liked. She saw the price. "Oh, heavenly father."

"Oh yeah, the house hunt." Joan was in the cubicle in a second, looking over Jesse's shoulders. "My eyes must be going bad. Tell me that does not say two million dollars."

"It doesn't," Jesse said with a sigh. "It says two-point-two million dollars."

"It's kind of small for that. How many . . ."

"Two bedrooms, one and a half baths." Jesse scrolled back. "This is hopeless. Why does everything cost a million dollars out here?"

"The way of the tech world. Find a technology hub, I'll

show you a cost of living that borders on the obscene. Haven't you heard, sister? We're all rich out here."

Jesse laughed. "I missed that memo. I should've guessed there would be a downside to living in a stunningly beautiful, mountainous paradise."

"Yeah, those are always cheap." Joan hopped backward on the counter next to the laptop. "Face it, Jesse. It's beautiful around here. The ocean is right at our doorstep, the mountains are everywhere we turn. The weather is perfect everyday. What did the *Mercury News* say? The median income here is almost sixty grand?"

"They left beat reporters who work at small weekly newspapers out of that survey."

"We would've dragged that median down too far, girl. Personally, I don't know what I would do if I didn't have Ray sharing the bills with me. You lucked out with the house-sitting deal."

Jesse knew she was right there. The first ad she'd responded to after moving to San Jose was for a couple looking for a house sitter through October, while they would be traveling in Latin America on a spiritual mission. It was a retired couple who had paid off the mortgage of their tiny two-bedroom over ten years ago. All they expected was six hundred dollars a month, which was half of any rent Jesse was finding for an apartment of comparable size in a quality neighborhood. She refused to test fate, and signed a short-term lease that day.

"I have to find a house by October, Joan." She clicked on another house she liked. "Or I'm on the streets. Look at this one. It's adorable, tiny. Just as small as the one I'm living in. Four hundred thousand dollars. Can you believe it?"

"It won't kill you to rent." Joan looked down at her

with a frown. "And don't start with some political theory on how the system of renting is designed to keep the poor poor. It's convenient for you."

"I want a house." Jesse bit her lower lip as she looked at the next listing. Another house, sold already. "Why don't they take them off the Internet when they sell them?"

"Calm down, stubborn. Besides, they sell so fast, they probably don't get time to take them off. Look, let's get something to eat and talk more about Sabrina. This is pretty interesting."

"You know what's even more interesting?" Luke Byrne, chief editor and owner of Silicon Valley Weekly strolled into the cube, resting his hands on his considerable belly. His face was red with sunburn from a recent extended beach visit.

"That would be actually working," he continued. "How about that? Interesting, huh, Joan?"

"We're on lunch, Luke." Joan always spoke with sarcasm to her boss. She knew he was fond of her, and she could get away with it. "Last I checked, that was our time."

"Whatever you say. Jesse, you got a second? We need to talk."

Jesse swung her chair around to face him. She hoped he was about to say what she thought he would. "Just say yes, and I'll give you as many seconds as you want."

"I'm your boss," he said. "You'll give me as many seconds as I want anyway. However, to save us both valuable time, yes. Your answer is yes."

Jesse threw her hands in the air. "All right! You won't regret this."

"I'd better not. Just make sure you do just like in your proposal, stretch it out. Don't give too much away. A new article every week, tie them together. And most important, don't repeat what we've all already heard."

"I know, I know. It was my proposal, remember? Don't worry, Luke, I've got this down. I've already done the basic groundwork."

"I can see that." He winked. "Good job. Go for it."

"Okay, what was that all about?" Joan asked as soon as Luke was gone.

"I told you already," Jesse asked. "I want to do a follow-up story on minority executives in Silicon Valley. The story came out a while ago, but what's been done about it? There still is a great disparity between Caucasians and minorities in management positions, in all positions within the technology center of the country. It's a big issue, and as diversity beat reporter, one I should be tackling."

"I see minorities around here all the time."

"That's not the issue, Joan. The African American and Latino people you see around here are not predominantly in the professional ranks. Those numbers are ridiculously low. There are a lot of Asians in the professional ranks, but still, when you look at the power structure, the senior management at the major companies, they aren't there either. It's really a big issue that I think a lot of people choose to ignore."

"Trying to save the world. That's your angle, right?"

"Information leads to knowledge. Knowledge is power."

"You know who you sound like?" Joan's eyes were compassionate.

"Who?"

"Yourself. Or at least the you that you explained to me you used to be." She frowned. "That sounded more confusing than it was. You know what I mean. The person you said you used to be before Henry."

The name made Jesse cringe. "I'm more than a feature article away from getting that person back."

"I think you underestimate yourself, girl. You spent a year in a controlling, dangerous relationship."

"Which shows how smart I am already."

"Don't say that. Even PhDs from Harvard can get caught up. The point is, you survived that relationship, found the strength to get out of it, and ended up the winner in this crazy stalking game he tried to play with you. You say you lost yourself because of this man, but I'd say you have more of yourself than you think."

Jesse smiled. "You're all right, Joan. You know that?"

Joan shrugged. "Yeah, I know. Just remember, so are you. Speaking of . . ."

"Don't ruin this by talking about a man now." Jesse clicked on the mortgage site she visited regularly. Just a reminder that she would never qualify for the loan she needed to buy a nice house. "You have me in your favor right now. Don't ruin it."

"I'm not. I'm just saying. You've built this wall around you because you're afraid of meeting another Henry. You could be passing up the guy who'll make you forget all the Henrys you've ever met."

Jesse sighed, the image of the handsome beach jogger coming to mind. But hadn't she been just as intrigued by Henry when she first saw him? Jesse had a heavy heart. It was still so deeply with her.

"I'm just not ready right now. I just wouldn't trust myself. I don't seem to have any type of litmus test for a man. If I feel it, I jump into it, and that caught up with me with Henry. Right now, I don't think I'd notice Mr. Right if he jogged right by."

* * *

"Hey, Dean. I only got a minute, but come on in and sit down." Cole waved to his friend, who helped himself to a seat.

Dean James sat down, eyeing the office. He took off his baseball cap, exposing his raisin brown bald head. He was wearing raggedy blue jeans and an untucked San Francisco 49ers T-shirt that stretched over a generous belly. A sharp contrast to Cole's pressed and neatly tucked white button-down and navy slacks.

"So what did you do with the info I got you on that lady?" Dean reached across the desk to grab a pen and began taking it apart. "That Sabrina."

Cole leaned back in his chair. He found Dean's need to take everything apart amusing. "I can't tell you that, Dean."

"What's up with you? I got you the info. What can you hide from me about it?"

"It's sensitive, Dean. I . . . We haven't decided what to do yet."

"Who is we?" Bored with the pen, Dean tossed it back on the table in three parts now.

"Me and my boss, Chris. We're grateful for your fast work though. One day turnaround. Wonderful job. Chris and I went over it, and it's all we need right now."

"She's the poster child for ordinary, average nobodies, man. Why would she be stealing from you?"

"Look around here." Cole's hand reached out toward the window overlooking downtown San Jose. "Some of the richest people out there look like they haven't showered in days or slept under a decent roof in years. You can't tell a shark by its appearance anymore. Look, I don't want to talk about her right now. Is she what you came by for?"

"No, man, I came by to see you," Dean said. "Don't you want an update on the party?"

"What party?"

Dean shook his head. "The Black Engineers of Silicon Valley Association, you idiot! The party my wife has been planning for five months. It's at your house. You said we could use it. You don't remember?"

"Of course I remember." Cole racked his brain. He belonged to the association of computer, civil, and general engineers in the area. There were a few of them that met regularly at each other's houses for events and networking. "Yeah, I remember that your wife volunteered my house for the summer banquet without talking to me first."

"Well, she could have if you'd ever show up for a meeting. That's not the issue anyway. The dinner is next week and she needs a key to your house to let the decorators in and set up for the caterers and party equipment."

Cole reached into his desk drawer for the extra key he kept for himself in case he forgot his own set. He tossed them at Dean. "Anything else? I've really got to get back to work."

"Man, we used to hang. You and Tracy, me and my wife. All that. Now, it's hard to remember if you're alive or not. You shuffle me out of your office like I was trying to sell you something. What's up?"

"We've talked about this before." Cole felt a little uncomfortable, knowing he didn't have much to say about it. He and Dean had known each other since Stanford. His friend deserved better than a brush-off. "I'm working on my new product. I don't have time for a life."

"Fine by me, but what does Tracy think of this?"

"Tracy is fine with what is going on." Cole didn't want to think about Tracy. He felt awkward talking about her at all. He couldn't remember the last time he thought about her in romantic terms. They spoke about once every two weeks now. It was going nowhere. He felt guilty, too, thinking of the woman from the beach again. That familiar stranger.

"Yeah, I'm sure she's just fine with it. Girls are so against that quality-time thing. It's probably a relief that you never even call her."

"Tracy has been in New York for almost two months now. You know she's working on that start-up."

"Yeah, but you guys are flying in for the weekends and stuff, right?"

Cole cleared his throat. "Dean, I'm really busy. I have got to . . ."

"Get to work. I know. Whatever, man. I've known you for what, eight years now? You've never been a party animal, but this is ridiculous. All for what? This product you say is going to make you a few extra bucks."

"A lot more than a few, Dean." Cole wished Dean could understand. He wasn't in this world. "This is going to make me a multimillionaire and CEO. It's going to be what makes my name in this industry."

"When was the last time you been to church, brother?"

"You asking me about church?" Cole laughed. "Mister On-parole-for-hacking-into-corporate-banks?"

"Hey." Dean raised his hands in the air. "I'm reformed. Besides, this is about you, not me. All I'm saying is everything I've gone through has taught me one thing. Money is not the bomb, like I thought it was. Don't get me wrong, I wish you well. I got a few shares of Netstyles myself. But a happy life requires balance. You got no balance."

"I'll give you a holler this weekend, Dean." Cole felt his mood darkening. He had to get back to work. It was the only thing that kept his life off his mind, kept that beautiful jogger off his mind.

"I won't hold my breath. Catch you later, man."

Cole tried to concentrate on his spreadsheet. Tracy. They weren't really a part of each other's lives anymore. He knew that. He had no life. No life, no woman, no friends anymore. He and Tracy were too hot or too cold while they were together. They either had a ball or fought like cats and dogs. He realized they stayed together because they were both too committed to their jobs to put in the real time required to find someone new, and neither of them would nag the other about the morality of their worship for the office.

When she had to leave for New York, Cole didn't feel as upset as he should have, and Tracy never once acted as if it was a hard choice to make. That was their relationship. It was sad and cold, he could admit that. He wanted happiness with a woman, a balanced life. But not now. Right now, it was all about alert.com. Everything was alert.com, and he wasn't going to let anything, including this Sabrina Joseph, whoever she was, get in the way.

"It's nice of you to come by." Felicia Joseph closed the door to Sabrina's house behind Jesse as she entered. "I was happy to get your phone call."

"I'm glad you were," Jesse said, taking a seat in the living room. It felt as eerie as the last time she'd been there, when Sabrina was recently dead. "I hope it's not too late. When Grace Lopez called me and told me you were here and had decided to have a wake for Sabrina, I was happy to hear it. I just thought I'd stop by to pay my respects in private."

Felicia sat down across from her. She was almost a replica of Sabrina, only a decade younger, thirty pounds lighter, and with a lot more composure. Her eyes were tired and red.

"I'm surprised that my sister has as many friends as she does. Or had. She was always a loner, awkward around people. Her neighbor really requested the wake. Said there were quite a few people in the neighborhood who would like to pay their respects."

"You look tired." Jesse felt compassion for the young woman. She thought of her own family when Grace had told her that Felicia was all that was left of this family. Her parents, who had found their souls in the 1960s and never accepted any other decade, were living in Seattle, Washington, doing God only knew what. They never married; it was too conventional for them. Her brother, Ash, was off taking pictures in Costa Rica. She rarely saw them, but loved them still, and was all the more grateful they were alive.

"I'm from Washington, D.C. This time-zone difference has got me all out of whack." She wiped away a strand of hair, the same color as her sister's, as it fell on her face. Her moves were slow, sad, unconscious. "Sabrina talked about her art class a couple of times over the phone. Said she loved it."

"She appeared to. She would be with us in the beginning of the class, but when she found her stride, she would zone out. She was like a bird flying with the paintbrush."

Felicia gave a half smile. "She loved art. I think it was the only thing in her life that fit right, you know? She was always confused, awkward, uncertain, a little off-center. But with art, she felt it."

"I know." Jesse was touched by Felicia's words. "I sort of feel that way, too. I guess that's why I liked her. I didn't know her that well, but we got along."

Felicia pointed to some of the paintings on the wall. "Are these from the class?"

Jesse recognized the paintings immediately. "Yes. Wow, it looks like she hung up every one she's done. She's pretty brave. I'm afraid to put mine up lest someone criticize them. It's silly, but Sabrina's paintings are really in contrast with the apartment. They're so scattered and abstract, but this place is so neat and tidy."

"Can you explain that?" Felicia looked confused.

"What do you mean?"

"Bless my sister's soul, but Sabrina was a slob. She was very messy. I'm sure you noticed that about her."

Jesse wasn't sure how to respond to that. "Well . . ."

"This place is immaculate. I know she didn't make enough to hire a cleaning lady. There isn't a speck of dust anywhere."

As if someone were trying to clean up after a struggle or erase any traces of fingerprints. Jesse thought this, but simply nodded to Felicia. "Well, that is a little strange. I don't know what could explain it."

"I'm so rude." Felicia stood up from the chair. "I haven't offered you anything to drink. I know it's pretty warm out there."

"Sit down. I don't want anything."

"Good. Because I wouldn't know where anything was anyway." She smiled a half smile.

Jesse smiled back, clearing her throat. "Felicia, have you spoken with the police?"

Felicia looked away for a moment. "About her death, yes. It looks like suicide. I have to agree. The medical examiner said there was an extremely high amount of a drug in her system. I don't remember what he called it. She had the cup of tea next to her bed. It was all in the cup and in the pot that was cooking the tea. Her life has been a mess recently, and I haven't been there for her like I could have. I feel awful."

"You can't blame yourself for this." Jesse wondered what kind of drug it was. Most drugs were easy to find now and could be bought on the Internet or even made from ingredients posted online.

"She tried to reach out to me when Mama died, but I was feeling sorry for myself. She tried to pour her heart out to me about her fiancé leaving her, but I'd just gotten engaged and I didn't want to hear it, so I sort of pushed her off. I just wanted to talk to people who could enjoy my happiness with me."

"I don't know what the call is on that," Jesse said. "But I just don't see her as a suicide threat. She seemed like a survivor. She seemed like someone who wore her bad fortune on her sleeve. Almost like a medal of some kind."

"That's the Sabrina I remember," Felicia added. "But we hadn't kept in contact for almost eight years. Separate lives, separate ends of the country, a couple of falling outs, the money thing. I hate to think of it."

"Then don't right now. You have too much to deal with anyway." Jesse decided not to probe further. Adding guilt to grief, the young girl was having a tough time of it.

"You think she was murdered?"

Jesse hesitated, but the look on Felicia's face said that she really wanted the truth, no niceties. "I can't say that I have anything to go on. I thinks there's just as much chance for murder as a suicide. Think of what she did for a living. She caught cheaters, testified against them in divorce court. I'm sure she cost plenty of men—and women for that matter—a lot of money in divorce settlements and alimony. And what about those people committing insurance fraud? What she catches them doing could send them to jail.''

"She had been in danger a few times. One time she called me for money to pay her hospital bill. She didn't have insurance at the time. She had gotten quite a few scratches and bruises in a car accident. This guy that claimed he couldn't move because he'd hurt himself at work was suing for about ten million. She caught him playing volleyball. Anyway, he caught her taking pictures and went after her. Chased her down the beach, and got in his car and tried to follow her. He actually got hurt more than her in the accident. But there you go.''

"Maybe you want to tell this to the cops," Jesse said. "I think it's worth looking into.''

"I'll think about it." She sighed. "Right now, I have to figure out what I'm going to do with all this stuff.''

"Look, Felicia, I'm gonna get going. You don't need me here right now bugging you about these things.'' Jesse stood up and headed for the door. "I don't know what I can do for you, but here's my card. Please call me if you have any questions you think I can answer. Or, if you want to talk about the police more.''

Felicia took the card. "Thanks. I'll give you a ring if I can before I leave. I have so much to clear up here, then the wake and I have to make arrangements to bring Sabrina and her things back home with me. It's so nice of you to stop by.''

"No problem." Jesse opened the door for herself. "I'm glad for the chance to get to meet you."

Jesse jolted back. The package delivery man almost hit her in the forehead with his fist as he stopped just short of knocking.

"I almost got you, lady," he said with a gold-toothed smile. "About to knock on this door right where your head is."

He was a young brother, cornrows to his neck, a gold chain hanging outside his brown uniform. Short and skinny.

"Can I help you?" Felicia asked as Jesse stepped aside.

"Package for Sabrina Joseph." He held up a bright yellow, thick, regular envelope–sized package.

"I'm her . . . sister." Felicia accepted the package. She looked it over. "The originating date on this was over a week ago. Why is it just now . . ."

"Ground shipping requested, lady," the man interrupted. "It's from Philly. It's kind of like regular mail, costs the same, except it can be tracked if it's lost or something." He accepted the signed form from Felicia. "Thanks, uhhh . . . Felicia. You two ladies have a nice day."

"Are you going to be okay?" Jesse asked. "That was unexpected."

"Life goes on." She placed the package on the stand next to the door. "The mail doesn't know what's happened to my sister. I'll open it later. I'm a little hungry right now. Thanks again for stopping by."

Jesse waited until the door was shut before she turned to walk away. As she stepped down the stairs, the sun, still fighting a now losing battle, hit her with what it had left. She shaded herself with her hands in time to see the package delivery man's truck almost crash into her car before maneuvering out of its space. As it drove off, her eyes were drawn to what it had been blocking.

It was a shiny, S-Series new black Mercedes sedan. Not a normal sight in this working-class neighborhood. Jesse was never a fan of what she considered symbols of capitalism and power. But it wasn't the car that made Jesse inhale sharply. She stopped, frozen in her tracks.

She could clearly see his well-chiseled face, strong jawline, and striking eyes. Even at this distance, with little light from the sun, his face had become so etched in her mind and her vision that it was unmistakable. It was him! The Jogger.

"Couldn't be," she whispered to herself, as she noticed he seemed just as floored to see her. Her knees weakened, her stomach pulled. An unconscious smile formed at the edges of her lips. She blinked, certain her eyes were deceiving her. When she still saw him, she felt a little dizzy.

Then she felt a chill trail her spine. This was too weird. How could this be? She wanted to believe in coincidences; her general disposition encouraged chance and fate. Especially with him. But something told her this was wrong and the smile quickly faded. Not just that she hadn't seen him for a month, then twice in just a matter of days, but the intensity on his face as he looked up at Sabrina's house, then back at her, told Jesse this was nothing even close to coincidence. Was he watching her? Following her?

Memories flooded back to her. Henry would wait outside her apartment in his car, just glaring at her. It sent shivers through her entire body. Of course he was sure to stay fifty feet away, as the restraining order directed, but just barely. He would stare and not say a word until she was about to get in her car. Then, he'd scream some type of threat or make a sexually offensive comment to her. It disturbed her neighbors, her friends, her coworkers. He stole her life.

Jesse felt the anger well up in her and assumed it was evident as The Jogger's expression went from some kind of wonder to apprehension. Quickly, he turned away and drove off. She followed the car with her eyes as her feet allowed her to move again. She felt her body loosen, her lungs breathe, her muscles let go. Jesse wasn't sure how long she stood at her car door before she got in. After getting over the shock of seeing him, she tried to think of other reasons for him to be there. She would buy anything at this point. Anything to believe he wasn't stalking her.

She wanted to convince herself she was being paranoid. Why would he stalk her? How would he even know her? She wished she had seen where he'd gone the other day. Into that building he stood in front of or somewhere else?

Maybe he'd seen her on her way to Sabrina's and thought to follow her, to finally approach her. But he didn't.

"There has to be some explanation," Jesse said to herself, her hands gripping the steering wheel so tightly her knuckles were turning colors.

She remembered the way he looked at the house. Sabrina's house. Was that it? Was he a friend? Was he one of the subjects of Sabrina's investigations? Had he known her? If so, how? How, and why be so mysterious about it? Jesse didn't know exactly what circumstances laid this man in her lap after all this time, but there was a point to it. Her next step was finding out what that was.

Cole headed back to his house, stunned. How could this be? It was her. Why there? As much as he tried to deny it at first, it was undeniable. Coming out of that house, Sabrina

Joseph's house. He didn't even know what to think or feel. He felt like he'd been hit with a brick, and part of him liked it. But this wasn't good. Couldn't be. He had to know who she was, how she knew Sabrina, and if she knew about him and Netstyles.

Cole had to think. What did he know of this woman besides the fact that she was the image of everything he imagined?

She was a reporter, right? He figured that much from what he had seen outside his office. Was she doing a story on Sabrina Joseph? Had Sabrina been selling Netstyles information to the press?

"This is too much," he said to himself, trying hard to concentrate on the road. He wasn't used to being caught this off-guard, this unaware of what to do next. That woman put everything out of whack in his life.

He tightened his grip on the steering wheel. Things had gone from bad to worse. The information had come quickly to him earlier today through Dean. He'd called early in the morning to tell Cole that Sabrina Joseph, the target of his investigation into who stole alert.com documents, was dead. Dean was a strange fellow who got his news from all sorts of unusual sources. Cole never questioned that, especially not when he could get some information from him.

Dean made a few phone calls to find out more and could only tell Cole it was considered suicide. But Cole had a feeling, and it was a bad feeling. He needed to know more. He needed to know if she still had those documents. If not, he was sure she wasn't a suicide victim. Someone had murdered her for it. It seemed farfetched to him at first, but not after a while. Not after thinking of all the things people did out here to be the first out with a product, the first to make millions before the market became saturated. He was no longer naïve about the cutthroat aspect of the technology software world.

He needed more information from Chris. Chris usually didn't lie to him, but he was keeping something from him now. If this Sabrina Joseph was after Netstyles because of Chris, there had to be more to it.

If that wasn't enough, now *she* was involved. He'd known from the first moment he saw her, she would be a part of his life some way or other. Then he'd thought he'd lost her forever. So now she was back and tied to his life in the least desirable way.

He hoped for a coincidence, that the reason was because it is such a small world. But something told him it was much more than that. And that was no good.

Chapter Three

Cole was at work early the next day. He was usually in the office around eight-thirty every morning. But he wasn't jogging today. He wasn't sure he wanted to anymore. At least not there. He felt like a fool going back there. Seeing that woman last night had really messed him up. He hardly slept thinking about her. It was becoming almost an obsession.

Chris had Debra call Cole into his office the second he arrived. Chris wanted an update, so Cole gave it to him. He was almost grateful for the distraction that updating Chris in his office provided. But now came another problem.

He wasn't sure what to make of Chris, looking at nothing in particular, brows narrowed upon hearing that Sabrina was dead. He simply sat there. What was going on?

"Aren't you concerned?" Cole asked.

"What, about the documents?" Chris asked. He hadn't shaven in a few days and the stubble made him look older, rugged.

"I don't know. Getting them is more complicated now."

"We need to know if she still has them."

"I'm getting a strong feeling, and it's that she doesn't. It's also that she was killed for those documents."

"I thought you said your friend Dean called it suicide."

"It's fishy."

"Forget the dead woman. Who cares? That's not important."

Cole was shocked. He'd known Chris was a little rough around the edges sometimes, but that was cold even for him.

"What's important," Chris went on, "is the product. We need to get into her place."

"You want to break into her home?" Cole asked. "That's illegal."

"She stole from us!"

Cole nodded. "But we don't have proof of that. We have to be more careful. I want to get to the bottom of this more than anyone, but I don't think breaking the law is the only answer."

"Screw the law," Chris said. "We can't bring the police into this. They're the biggest leaks around. We have to be the law ourselves. Get your buddy to do it. He's an ex-con after all."

"Look, Chris. Dean is a reformed hacker, not a home burglar. This is not his game. Besides, I'd never put him at risk like that." Cole had to check himself. He believed those words, didn't he? He couldn't begin to question it, but he did. No, of course not. He'd never ask anyone, let alone a friend, to do something illegal just to make money.

Chris backed down a bit, as he always did when Cole put his foot down. He didn't challenge his number one man too much. There was a lot to lose if Cole decided to take his talent elsewhere. Cole knew that Chris was aware of the ten calls a week he received from headhunters promising Cole the world if he would jump ship.

"Fine, Cole," he went on, standing up. He glanced around his sparsely decorated office. "However, we have to get whatever information she had on me and alert.com. It's not ready to roll out yet. There are some up-front advertisers we still have to deal with."

"Let's call Paul in," Cole said, reaching for the phone. "This is what we pay him for."

"No." Chris reached for the phone and pulled it out of Cole's grasp. "He got the advertisers on board. That was his job. You and I can take it from here."

Cole rolled his eyes. He was tired of the pissing contest between Paul and Chris. They couldn't stand each other. "Paul is business development and he's good."

"Not as good as you were, Cole. You have to admit that. You were better than anyone at pulling them in for the final commitment. We can't take the chance that someone else will jump on all our hard work and get the step on us. Or even worse, get the product out so soon after us, we don't have time to dominate the market."

Cole knew he was right. He could not let this happen! He'd worked too hard for this. "I'll figure something out. I think I have an angle on Sabrina."

"What?"

"There was this woman coming out of her house late last night. I drove by to see if anyone in particular was looking for what we're after. The woman had this look on her face when she saw me. She knows something, Chris. I'm certain if I can get close to her, I might even get into that house. I think she's a reporter, so I'm sure I can find her. I have a lead with a friend at Top Pressure. Well, an acquaintance at least.''

Chris's entire demeanor calmed. ''I want everything Sabrina was working on. Everything.''

Cole nodded in agreement. He didn't want to believe Chris was holding out on him. Their entire relationship was based on trust and mutual benefit. He couldn't doubt that.

''I know you'll do it, Cole.'' Chris made the fingers between the buttons move again. ''Everything you set your mind to, you blow it out of the water. You leave nothing incomplete, no stone unturned. We just have to make it fast.''

Cole wasn't listening to Chris anymore. He was thinking about her. Her, and how he could find out who she was, what she knew, and if she could lead him to those documents. If it wasn't too late.

''There are a lot of people here,'' Joan said as she leaned over to Jesse. ''I didn't know Sabrina would have this many friends. She seemed like a two-or-three-friends-in-the-whole-world type of gal.''

Jesse was happily surprised to see almost thirty people at the wake for Sabrina. Some of them she recognized from the art class. She had called their teacher, who promised to leave a phone message for everyone in the class, but Jesse wasn't sure they would respond. Maybe it was the location, a funeral home right in the middle of San Jose, easily accessible traffic-wise, close to where most of them lived. Others she had no idea. She and Joan had arrived early, spending time with Felicia, who then said a few words before others lined up to show their respect. Now that the crowd was thinning, Jesse was getting a good look around.

With all due respect to Sabrina, she was not the first thing on Jesse's mind. He was, and Jesse's radar was out for him the second she arrived. But he hadn't showed, and Jesse was feeling a sincere level of disappointment. Over the past couple of days she had decided that Sabrina was her link to him, and he would appear.

"Do you think he's here?" Joan asked, taking a sip of punch as the crowd dwindled down.

"Who?" Jesse's eyes widened. How did Joan know about The Jogger?

"The murderer!" Joan sighed impatiently. "Where is your mind today? Look, Jesse. If you're going to be a real journalist, you have to be always on the lookout. You think Sabrina was murdered, then wouldn't her funeral be a prime place to spot her murderer?"

Jesse nodded. "I know that. I've been looking, but I don't recognize anyone but Grace and some of the girls from the class. I think I . . ."

He entered as if in a staged hero scene, walking into the room with mastery and presence. The Jogger. Everyone's eyes turned to him. The women smiled and the men took mental notes. Jesse felt that familiar mix of fear and excitement that only he seemed to bring out in her. Seeing him there answered a lot of questions for Jesse, but raised even more. Still, what hit her most was how good he looked. Not drop-dead gorgeous, but so utterly charming.

He was in a business suit, hands crushed into his pockets, eyes directly on . . . Jesse stepped a little farther to the right to see what it was his eyes were so intent on. The young man, caramel complexion, medium build, dressed like a Lands' End cover boy, was looking back at him, and was looking scared. His eyes would dart toward Cole, then away, then back. Jesse had noticed him from before. He'd only showed up ten minutes or so ago. He'd kept to the back, as if he wasn't sure he wanted to be there. He wasn't talking to anyone, just sipping a cup of juice. Jesse could swear she saw his hand shaking.

Her attention turned back to The Jogger, who was reaching into his pocket. He pulled out his cellular phone and darted into the corner of the room to talk in private. His eyes sent occasional daggers to the other man.

"What's up?" Joan tugged at Jesse's arm. "Why did you stop in midsentence? What are you looking at?"

"I'm on the lookout, like you said." Jesse leaned over as if what she said was a secret. "I'm on to something. I'll meet you back at the paper."

"Need help?"

Jesse shook her head. "Catch you later."

"You're makin' me proud."

The young man was too preoccupied with The Jogger to notice Jesse as she approached him. She had to tap him on the shoulder to get his attention.

"Are you a friend of Sabrina's?" she asked. He looked to be in his mid-twenties, with light eyes and small features that made him look a little annoyed all the time.

"Yes, well, kind of." He didn't appear to be interested in talking to anyone.

"So did I. We had a class together." Jesse held out her hand. "Jesse Grant."

"Paul Brown." He shook her hand with a nod. He placed his cup down. "It was nice meeting . . ."

Jesse stepped to the left to keep him from leaving. She leaned in. "So what's the problem with the suit?"

He looked at her, his eyes widened. He glanced around quickly. "What are you . . ."

Jesse tilted her head to the side in a no-nonsense gesture. "Don't bother with that. He's got you ready to crawl out of your skin. Gives me the creeps, too. Who is he?"

"He's my boss," he answered after a second hesitation. "I didn't expect to see him here. I shouldn't have come."

Jesse was excited with the anticipation of getting information on him. "Where do you work?"

Paul looked her up and down quickly. "Who did you say you were?"

"I'm a friend of Sabrina. I know she was working on a lot of cases that were pretty dangerous. Personally, I gotta say I think she was murdered. Don't you?"

Paul appeared surprised. "Murdered? Well, I mean . . . everyone said it was . . ."

"Suicide." Jesse turned her head slightly and lost her thought, realizing that he was off the phone now, staring at her, at the two of them from a distance. He wasn't at all pleased. "I . . . I know that. But I . . . don't . . . I don't think so."

"I didn't know Sabrina well enough to really talk about any of that." Paul was becoming restless now that Cole's attention was on him again. "We were just acquaintances. We worked out at the same time. You know, at Rock's Gym. Sometimes we would talk. She was a nice girl. I called to see why she hadn't been working out recently and found this out. Look, Cole is driving me crazy staring at me. I've got to go."

"Cole?" A name! Jesse couldn't believe how much excitement it bought her to know his . . . Wait a second, she thought. That name sounded familiar even though she was sure it shouldn't. "Cole who?"

"Cole Nicholson. He's the suit." He stepped again to the left. "Like I was saying, it was nice meeting you Jesse, but I . . ."

Jesse gently grabbed at his arm just as he was about to leave. "Wait a second, Paul. Who is Cole Nicholson? The name is familiar to me."

"Did Sabrina tell you about him?" He eyed her strangely, as if aware this was an unusually evasive conversation for two practical strangers.

"Maybe," Jesse said. "But help me out."

"Do you know about Netstyles?"

Jesse was shaking her head no at first, but then it came to her. It all came to her and the connection floored her. "Netstyles is the software company. Cole Nicholson and Chris something-or-other."

"Chris Spall. Yeah, you know them. That's Cole." He pulled his arm away. "I've got to get back to work."

"Why are you so scared?" Jesse asked, trying to keep her head together as she realized the amazing coincidence. "Don't try to hide it, Paul. You're frightened of him. He can't be such a slave driver that you can't attend a friend's funeral."

The challenge to his pride kept him from leaving. He looked back at Jesse. "I'm not frightened. I just didn't . . . I didn't know he knew her. He shouldn't know her at all. I didn't expect to see him. I'm not sure what . . . I just got to go."

"Paul," Jesse called after him, but he was gone. What was going on? This man, who had invaded her life in such a fleeting way months ago, creeping into her dreams, was connected to Sabrina's private investigation. That was why he was outside her house.

Jesse knew it was a small world, but she thought this was ridiculous. She didn't even have time to enjoy knowing his name, she was so eager to find out how he knew Sabrina. How did he know she was investigating Sabrina's death? She had to find out, but the thought of actually approaching him, something she never had the courage to do before, made her stomach tighten. After all this time. But there was no turning back now. She turned, starting for him, when someone grabbed her arm and kept her from moving.

Her heart stopped and the world disappeared. It was Cole holding on to her. He was looking directly into her eyes. He was so close, only a foot from her.

Cole tried to keep his focus, in spite of the proximity.

He had been staking out Sabrina's funeral for anyone that would possibly benefit from alert.com secrets. Anyone that he would recognize. He didn't question how Dean got the information on where and when the wake would be. Cole was counting on her murderer, if there was one, to show up for one of two reasons. One was guilt, hoping to redeem himself. The other was to avert suspicion. If her murderer was close to her, not showing up at her funeral would raise suspicion in other people that knew Sabrina.

When a familiar woman showed up, Cole knew she must be The Jogger. She was gorgeous in a navy blue rayon short dress. Her hair was glossy and flowing back. He'd taken a few pictures before she'd gone inside. He'd wanted to follow her, certain that their circumstances meant they were destined to meet, but instead kept to his job.

Paul's appearance shocked him, floored him, and compelled him to follow him inside. He quickly called Chris with an update, and was urged not to confront Paul. Not yet. But then, she was talking to him. Cole's determination to get answers finally overcame his speechlessness as he stood so close to her.

"Who are you?" he asked, looking into her large, dark eyes. A question he'd wanted answered for months now.

Jesse swallowed, feeling only his hand on her arm and the heat from it. She couldn't believe how excited she felt, as if a bolt of lightning was flowing from him to her.

"Who are you?" he repeated, the innocence of her face melting his resolve. "And how do you know Paul Brown and Sabrina Joseph?"

"You sure are full of questions, Cole Nicholson." Jesse tried to pull herself together, jerking her arm away. It was the only way she could get her mind back.

Cole was taken aback. "How do you know who I am?"

He was trying to get the upper hand, making Jesse want to play coy, although she wasn't sure she had it in her at that moment. She would try anyway. "Of course I know you, Cole. You're Paul's boss. You weren't expected here. I'm surprised. . . ."

"How do you know Paul?" How did she know so much?

"Paul and I are friends," she lied. "Through Sabrina, you know. The reason we are all here. How do you know her, by the way?"

Cole looked her over. She looked sexy even though her dress was relatively conservative. She had a natural sex appeal that would come through even in a T-shirt and baggy pants. But she wasn't fooling him. She was trying to, but she wasn't succeeding.

"Are you trying to do a story about this?"

"About what, Mr. Nicholson? Sabrina Joseph committed suicide. You know differently?"

"You're slick, Ms. . . ."

"Grant," she answered. "Jesse Grant."

"Ms. Grant," he continued, finally happy to add a name to the face that was etched in his head. "But you don't know what you're dealing with. Whatever Paul is up to . . ."

"Paul isn't up to anything," she said, not sure at all what she was talking about. But neither did he, so she felt safe. If only he weren't so close. "He's here to pay his respect to a friend. They worked out together. You, on the other hand, seem to be here to harass people."

Cole laughed, not believing for a second in the coincidence that Paul was a friend of Sabrina's. "Harass? Please. Paul is a coward. He would consider anyone asking him a question harassment. Still, he's smart and I don't trust him."

Jesse remembered Sabrina's notes on Netstyles. Lies, theft, and cover-up. "What reason would you have not to trust him?"

Cole wasn't going to give this reporter, no matter how beautiful she was, more information than he wanted her to have. He wasn't sure why he'd told her as much as he had already. Yes, he was. Finally talking to her, no matter what the topic, left his sensibility behind. She knew too much already. "What has he told you about Sabrina?"

"I told you. They used to work out together." Jesse knew she was making him irritated, frustrated, although it wasn't easy to tell. She was engrossed in the topic of conversation, but in the back of her mind, she still couldn't believe she was actually talking to him! Something about this was so unreal to her, but she had to concentrate and never let him know how much this affected her. "It's a very innocent relationship. You're the one who doesn't belong here."

"You don't know that," he said. Jesse Grant. He'd remember that name. He knew what he had to do next. "You don't know a lot that you're pretending to know. You're being a nosy reporter, but this isn't a feature story for your lifestyle section. You need to stay out of this."

"Out of what?" Jesse felt herself getting more aggressive. Finally. "I'll have you know that I'm not here as a reporter. And I work as a diversity reporter on serious issues, not lifestyles, by the way. Sabrina was a friend of mine, and I want to know who murdered her."

"You just said she committed suicide." She was a pretty feisty little thing, but he could handle her. Besides, he liked that. "What made you change your mind?"

Jesse raised her chin stubbornly. "I didn't. I was just testing you."

"It's not wise to test me, Jesse." He wanted to be angry with her, but instead he was incredibly turned on.

Jesse lost her composure for a moment. The power in his voice when he'd spoken just now sent a tingle through her. She swallowed, trying to recover. "I want to know what is going on."

Cole believed her and wanted to tell her everything. But no. He couldn't. Not about this.

"I'm sure you're genuinely concerned, but you need to stay out of it. Everything will be resolved soon. If it even was murder." He wanted to stay, but he knew telling Chris that Paul was at Sabrina's funeral had Chris in a panic. He had to get back to the office before Chris upset everyone.

His movements were confusing to Jesse. Did he want to leave or not? She didn't want him to, but could never tell him that. She had his name. To ask for more than that at this point seemed too much.

"I don't like being told what to do," she said, placing her hands on her hips.

Cole smiled. "I figured that about you. You have a nice day, Jesse Grant. I have a feeling we'll meet again."

As he walked away and out of the room, Jesse bit her lower lip in anticipation. Yes, that had really happened. Finally meeting him had been more than enough of a jolt to her system. She was happy at least that he wasn't stalking her. No more memories of Henry popping up. That was the good news.

The bad news was that he was Cole Nicholson of Netstyles, and his name had been on that sheet of paper that Sabrina left in her car. She'd been investigating Chris Spall, but Cole's activities had been followed as well.

"Lies, theft, and cover-up," she whispered to herself. Was Cole connected to Sabrina's murder? Was she even certain it was murder?

"What did you say?"

Jesse swung around to face Felicia Joseph, who was standing behind her holding a gray and white backpack. "Felicia."

"What did you just say?" Felicia asked.

"Nothing. I was talking to myself. How are you holding up? Are you making it through the day?"

Felicia shrugged. "I'm happy to see this. There were a lot of people here. You know, I had no idea that Sabrina had so many . . . Well, I'm just glad everyone could come. They've been so nice. I hate to push everyone out, but my flight is at three. Sabrina and I have to go back home."

Jesse placed a hand on her shoulder. "Everyone here is glad that you decided to do this. You didn't have to."

"I owe her that. I should've been there for her more than I was. Maybe if I had been, this wouldn't have happened."

"Felicia." Jesse's tone was compassionate, tender. "I don't have any proof, but I don't think Sabrina killed herself. I know you don't agree."

"I think maybe you're not so farfetched. Or maybe I'm not thinking straight." She reached into the backpack and pulled out an envelope, handing it to Jesse. "I don't want to believe she was murdered. You know, I'd actually rather believe it was suicide and take the blame than think that someone . . . you know."

"What is this?" Jesse opened the envelope and began reading the letter. "Congratulations, you've chosen the premier program with Branton Travel."

"That was what that delivery man was dropping off when you were leaving my sister's house a few days ago. I'm wondering why my sister would be taking a trip to the Cayman Islands if she was planning on killing herself."

"That's a good question." Jesse's conviction was strengthening. "According to this, she was supposed to be going next week."

"She could've been deciding whether or not to kill herself or get away, but chose the former," Felicia said. The look on her face said that she didn't really believe that.

Jesse thought it over. "Doesn't make sense. Think about it. The date on this itinerary says that these plans were made, or at least paid for, less than three weeks ago. That was pretty close to her death. If someone is that close to committing suicide, a Caribbean getaway is not an alternative. It's too far on the other end of the spectrum."

"I'm giving this to you." She handed Jesse the backpack. "These are all her files from whatever she was working on. You want to find out what happened, don't you?"

"Yes, I do."

"Well, go ahead and dig in. I would, you know. I mean,

I love my sister. I want the truth to come out, but I have to go home. I feel alone here. I need to be with my fiancé and my cousins. They're my family, and I can't really stay here right now."

"I understand," Jesse said. "I'll keep you updated."

"I put all my contact information in that bag." She sighed. "You don't think bad of me for leaving, do you?"

Jesse answered her with a hug. She knew the woman was torn. She loved her sister, but they weren't close. She shouldn't be expected to feign a relationship that didn't exist even though she was genuinely grieving.

Back in her car, Jesse placed the backpack in the passenger seat, wondering where she would start.

"The travel agent," she said to herself. "That was the convincing part for me, so that's where I'll start for now."

She looked around, wondering if she'd see him. But he was gone. For now.

Cole Nicholson. That was his name. Jesse felt silly saying it over and over again in her mind. She'd have to find out more about him first, and then how he was connected to Sabrina. She wondered if he was dangerous. She wondered if he thought she was. She wondered if he was repeating her name in his head over and over again right now.

With a not-so-happy feeling, she wondered why he asked her who she was. After all, he knew who she was. From the beach. He knew her all too well, and she him. Why didn't he mention the beach, the morning jogs? Why didn't she? The next time they met, would they pretend that they'd never seen each other there? Were their silent encounters so affecting that they chose to ignore them? Or maybe their pride kept each of them from being the first to say something.

She would see him again and soon. Jesse already knew

how she would get to him. Cole Nicholson played it cool today, but she wasn't intimidated by him. He was Paul's boss, not hers. Jesse felt a great energy take over her. She was feeling more like her old self.

Cole Nicholson. Cole Nicholson. Cole Nicholson.

Chapter Four

Jesse Grant. Jesse Grant. Jesse Grant.

Sitting at his desk, Cole studied the information before him. Dean certainly did his stuff fast. He had called Dean after the wake and asked for everything on Jesse Grant, a reporter in the area. That was all he had given him, but it was enough for Dean, who had five pages of information on her waiting for Cole when he showed up at his office the next morning.

"So this one isn't going to end up a suspicious suicide victim, is she?"

Cole looked up from the papers to Dean. "Not funny, man."

Dean was leaning against the wall, looking down at Cole in his chair. "I wasn't joking."

Cole realized he wasn't. He placed the paper on the desk.

"I swear to you, Dean. I didn't have anything to do with that woman's death."

"I never thought you did. But you're connected somehow. I can tell you think that."

Cole shook his head, turning his back to Dean. "We don't know that. She was a private investigator, remember?"

"Who stole from you." He walked around to the other side of the desk. "From Chris."

"Don't start on Chris."

"You think he walks on water."

"No, I don't. But he's not a murderer."

Dean leaned back in the chair. "Isn't that what they always say about murderers?"

Cole made a low growling sound.

"Fine," Dean said. "We're off Saint Chris. How about this Midwest-bred pretty? Who is she and how does she tie into all of this?"

"I don't know yet." Cole looked at the papers sitting in front of him. "This is more personal than professional, if you want the truth."

"For once it would be nice."

Cole squinted at him with a half smile. "I haven't been able to get this woman off my mind. I've got Chris having a panic attack every half hour and my own workload. I don't know what to do about Paul."

"That brother down the hallway here? How is he in this?"

"Not important," Cole said. "Bottom line is I have this product and I've got to protect it."

"At all costs?"

Cole nodded. He refrained from mentioning Chris's suggestions that they use illegal methods to go about it.

"Does Ms. Grant from Chicago fit in at all?"

"She does. I don't know how exactly, but she does and I'm going to find out." Cole briefly looked through the papers.

Her full name was Jessica Elizabeth Grant, she was twenty-eight, with parents who had never married and were well-known community activists. Her brother was a geologist with an arrest record for protesting everything from the rain forest to fur.

"Bunch of hippies," he said with a laugh. He got that about her. The way she moved when she jogged, when she walked, even when she was standing still. She was a free spirit. He envied that type of person. He'd always been in such a rush to achieve, a laid-back style was never an option for him.

"You do realize I'm still in the room, don't you?" Dean asked.

Cole smiled. "Almost forgot."

Dean's expression turned serious. "This girl really does something for you, huh? Well, I would be happy for you if it wasn't for Tracy. You do remember her?"

Cole sighed. "There's nothing between me and Jesse Grant. Hell, there's nothing between me and Tracy."

"You know she was never my favorite person," Dean said. "Too beautiful, sort of cold, and always planning."

"Hey," Cole said. "She's a nice woman."

"Oh, yeah. That's some way to describe your lover. A nice woman. Sounds like you're talking about a stranger."

"Lately it's been feeling like we are strangers."

"Then why don't you end it?"

"I want to, Dean. Only, this product. All of it. I just don't . . ."

"You just don't want to face the drama." Dean stood

up with a stretch. "But that's not fair to her. Besides, I don't think there will be any. Not that you aren't a stud or anything. I just get the feeling that she won't be devastated."

"Thanks for the compliment," Cole said. "See ya around."

"Pick up a phone for something other than a favor every now and then, huh?"

Cole nodded, feeling ashamed. He waited until Dean was gone before returning to the papers.

Thanks to technology, he now knew just about everything there was to know about Jesse Grant. Where she lived, where she worked, what her credit rating was, that she had applied for a home loan and had been denied. Everything except how she knew Sabrina Joseph, which was what he wanted to know the most.

He was frustrated, and getting a little concerned. He didn't want to believe that Sabrina's death was connected to alert.com, but he knew it wasn't out of the ballpark. She was a private investigator, after all, and one of her other cases could have caught up with her at the most inconvenient time. Not that there was a convenient time for murder or suicide, whichever it was in this case.

Then still, there was the reason behind her stealing the documents in the first place, which Chris claimed not to know. Cole owed him the benefit of the doubt. There had to be another . . .

"Thinking up a new product to create a software monopoly and keep the little man from rising up?"

Cole's surprise at seeing Jesse in his doorway quickly changed to pleasure. She looked like a breath of fresh air, all peach and tanned. That sarcastic little smile brought out that dimple he had missed seeing so much.

He leaned back in his chair, trying to appear cool and unaffected. "I am the little man in this industry. At least for now."

"But this, whatever you're concentrating so hard on, is going to change that." Jesse welcomed herself into the office, taking pleasure in the positive response his eyes gave her. She walked without any predetermined direction to the chair across from him, tape recorder in hand.

"Yes, it is," he answered with skepticism. "But don't expect to hear what it is."

"I would expect no such thing." She wriggled in her seat. "Enough about me. Today is your lucky day, Mr. Nicholson."

He raised a brow. "I figured that the second you walked in here."

Jesse smiled wryly. "This is strictly professional. I've chosen you as my first subject for my new story."

"What makes me so worthy of this?" he asked. "And how did you get up here anyway? You don't have security access."

She tilted her head with a smirk. "Please. I've wormed my way in and out of tighter places than Netstyles. If you bothered to hire anyone over the age of twenty-five here, it might be a little harder for me to outsmart them."

Cole laughed. He always imagined her having a bit of a spicy mouth. "I asked two questions, Ms. Grant. You only answered one."

"You're a smart one," she said, making certain not to underestimate him. He looked like your typical tech exec, too rich for his age, not socially dominant. Too busy being smart for that. But it seemed Cole was the exception. Rich and socially capable.

"And you're worthy," she continued, "because you are

in a prime and rare position. You're a top-level executive in Silicon Valley who happens to be African American. In your unique position, I'm sure you would be open to sharing what you can for . . ."

"For your paper?" he asked.

"Yes." Jesse sensed his annoyance, and wondered why. "For the *Silicon Valley Weekly*. I'm the diversity beat reporter. I'm doing a follow-up series on all the issues that came up a few years ago when the lack of minorities in tech industries was made public. I'm trying to find out what, if anything, has changed. How do people in the industry feel the publicity has affected them? What still needs to be done?"

"You sure you can handle all of that? There's enough information there to keep you busy for a year at least."

"If so, then that's what it will take." Jesse shrugged. "I'm committed to getting this information out. Can I depend on your help?"

"A social warrior," Cole said. "Haven't come across one of you in a while."

Jesse felt her temperature rising a bit. "Are you making fun of me, Mr. Nicholson?"

"No." He noticed her sitting up straight. She didn't take any mess. "Calm down, Jesse. I can call you Jesse, can't I?"

"Not yet."

"Fine, Ms. Grant. All I'm saying is, everyone in the valley is so set on making millions on the Net, that there doesn't seem to be a lot of room for activism."

"I disagree. I see it happening a lot. You saw what Peter Jackson's group was doing outside of Top Pressure's offices, didn't you?"

Remembering that day, when he'd first seen her again

after all that time, Cole didn't have a response. An awkward silence fell between them. His eyes lowered to his desk, and he suddenly realized that Jesse's entire life was on paper right in front of her. He quickly slipped the papers in the folder and slipped it into his drawer.

"You sure are protective," Jesse commented, her curiosity aroused.

"Everything here is proprietary information, Jesse." He stood up and walked around his desk, leaning back on it. "Now back to your story. I don't feel as if I can help you that much. Right now, I'm in the middle of a lot of . . ."

"Alert.com?" Jesse was surprised at the look of alarm on his face as she spoke those words. Alarm with a sharp tinge of anger.

"How do you know about that?" Cole felt his blood rush and bells go off. "What do you have?"

"It's my turn to say, 'Calm down'," Jesse said. "I just wanted to . . ."

"What do you know about it?" He now saw her connection to Sabrina was relevant. "Do you have the papers?"

"I . . ." Jesse didn't know what to say. "I just know that alert.com is something you're working on."

"Give them to me." He held his hand out, even though he knew she had nothing on her. "Give me the file she has on Chris and my company."

Jesse stood up, angry now herself. "Don't make demands on me, Mr. Nicholson. I don't know what Sabrina was . . ."

"She was investigating my boss, Chris Spall. I need those files, Jesse."

"We have to make a deal." Jesse couldn't believe she was doing this. The look on his face was almost desperate. She was probably in over her head. She should have just gotten out of there, but she needed this story. And she was more excited than she'd been in a long time. "I'll give them to you."

"A deal!" He laughed sarcastically. "Sabrina stole those papers from us."

"There are no papers," Jesse said. "There are no Netstyles papers in her file. I don't know what you're talking about."

Cole tried to calm down, realizing both of their voices were raised. "What is in there then?"

"Just her own notes on steno paper. I'm trying to find out if her murder—"

"Are we going to go over that again? For all you know, she committed suicide," He didn't believe his own words. "The police said that's what it was. Overdose."

"I don't believe that," Jesse said, "and neither do you. I can read people, and even though you put up a good front, you didn't believe one word you just said."

"What's in the file, Jesse?" She was staring at him, and Cole realized she could get him to tell her anything.

"A deal." Jesse placed nervous hands on her hips. She was pushing it.

Cole took a deep breath. He had no time for this. At least this was a clue. He would appease her. "What deal?"

"I give you Sabrina's file on Netstyles and I get to interview you for an in-depth article, and you let me use your contacts for more information."

Cole gritted his teeth, making a growling sound. "I don't have the time to be your eternal subject."

"Well, then." She slid her tiny recorder in her back pocket, twirling her keys around her index finger. "You have a nice day, Mr. Nicholson."

"Jesse!" He frowned at her haughty turn. "Fine. I can

give you an interview and give you some contacts. Give me the file."

"I don't have it on me now, but I'll get it to you later today." She held her hand out to him. "We can shake on it, or you can write it up."

He took her hand, shaking it vigorously. Her skin was soft, her fingers thin. He was frustrated, but not too frustrated to realize he was touching her.

Jesse pulled her hand away, swallowing hard. What was that about? A handshake could cause her stomach to twirl like that?

"What's in it?" Cole sat back down. "The file."

Jesse returned to her chair as well. She needed to sit down. "I *told* you, her notes. She's been keeping an eye on Chris, a little bit on you."

"Me?" Cole thought this was all about Chris. But if alert.com came into play, he would have to be involved. "What for?"

"You surprised at that?"

"No. I'm not surprised at much. I just want to get my hands on that file. Jesse, no matter what you think of what happened to Sabrina, I did not have anything to do with it."

Jesse paused as she looked into his hazel eyes, those eyes she had missed glancing at in the early mornings on the beach. "I believe you. But do you know who might have?"

"No." He wasn't willing to give anything there.

"Chris was her target. Her notes focus on her observations of his behavior, daily practices, financial stuff that would be public knowledge. It talks about a product called alert.com. What is that?"

"I can't tell you that."

"Aw, come on. I told you so much."

"That wasn't part of the deal." She was a pushy one.

Jesse sighed. "Well, what about Chris Spall? I did some research on your company earlier this morning and he's number one to your number two. You would know him better than anyone. Did he kill her?"

"No." Cole spoke with as much conviction as he could. "I've known Chris for three years, and since day one he has shown integrity. He's a ruthless businessman, but where morals are concerned, he's a family man and does a lot for charity."

Jesse wasn't convinced, but Cole seemed to be, so she left that alone for now. "So, can we get started?"

Cole laughed. "Do you actually think I have that type of free time? That I would drop everything I was doing to give impromptu interviews?"

"Just a few questions."

"Not now." As much as he wanted her to stay, this new break in the document saga had to be handled. "My admin is outside the office. Set something up with her and bring the file back here as soon as you can today."

"No." Jesse wasn't falling for that.

"What?" Cole felt his fingers gripping his pen tightly. She was frustrating. "We have a deal."

"I want to see good faith."

"Good faith!" He threw his hands in the air. "I agreed to this, didn't I?"

"And I told you what was in the files. I want a few questions answered."

He waved his hand away. "Three questions."

Jesse smiled victoriously as he appeared thoroughly annoyed. She pulled out her tape recorder and placed it on the desk. Taking her time, she leaned back in the chair. "Now, Mr. Nicholson."

"Cole. My father is Mr. Nicholson."

"Cole." Jesse nodded. "Where were you when all the publicity about the whitewash of Silicon Valley got started? Not in general, but when it started getting nationwide attention that the high-tech industry was so lily-white?"

Cole saw a sparkle in her eye. She meant it. She cared. "It was well known to those of us in the industry that we were way underrepresented. However, when it started to gain national attention, Jesse Jackson getting involved and all that, that was about three years ago. I was with a major computer company, Jennet-Dackard in San Francisco. I was a senior product analyst."

"Do you feel that's where you should have been? I mean, you had a bachelor's from the University of California at Berkeley and an MBA from Stanford, with a good bit of experience under your belt for this industry. Do you feel Jennet-Dackard was promoting you appropriately?"

"How do you know so much about me?" he asked with all hypocrisy.

"I'm a journalist, remember?" Jesse would never admit how much personal satisfaction she got out of finding out information on the man whose background she had pretty much made up in her mind. "I always study my subjects. The question, Cole."

"I don't believe in complaining, Jesse."

"Complaining? Are you saying that pointing out discrimination is complaining?"

"I'm saying crying over spilled milk is complaining. Jesse, there was discrimination at Jennet-Dackard just like at every other company in the world. I had to work twice as hard as everyone else to get half the recognition. All of my mistakes were attributed to my race, rather than human error. Everything I did wrong stuck. So what? That's what we all face. I was paid well and never once let anyone take credit for my products. I wasn't unhappy at JD. When this media frenzy came out, I was happy for a lot of people who needed it. I was on my way to Netstyles to work for a man who didn't give a damn what my skin color was."

"So you just walked away from it? From the rest of them?"

She made him feel uncomfortable now. "Sorry, Jesse. That's your fourth question. The deal was three. Get me the file and I'll give you some more for your story."

Jesse rolled her eyes. She thought to argue, but didn't. "How do I know you'll keep cooperating after I give the file to you?"

"I'm not a liar, Jesse." Besides, he was warming to the idea of seeing her regularly. "We shook on it. I'll cooperate."

"I hope you do a better job than you have so far. Your answers are pretty weak and uninspiring."

"I beg your pardon?" He eyed her intently. "When did insults become a part of our agreement?"

"You're one of a few, Cole. You're next in line for the CEO job aren't you? That's what that recent *Mercury News* article said. How many African Americans, or minorities in general, are in your position? Your comments should be inspiring, encouraging. Your involvement should be real."

"My comments and involvements should be how I want them to be, Jesse. And this interview is over for now. I have a meeting with the sales team in five minutes."

He stood up again, heading for the door. He watched as Jesse purposefully took her time, reaching for her recorder, her keys. She slowly got up and sauntered to the door.

"I'm not a pushover," she said. "I won't let you push me off."

"I never took you for a pushover from the first moment I saw you, Jesse."

Their eyes caught. They both knew what he meant. At the beach, the first moment they saw each other. Jesse was touched but it made her feel uncomfortable, not in control. So he wasn't going to say anything about the beach. She was just supposed to infer it.

"Whatever," was all she said before heading out of the office and straight for the secretary. Jesse could only hope she was walking straight. Inside, she was like jelly.

Cole watched her walk off, enjoying the view immensely. So this was Jesse Grant. Frustrating, but overall better than he even imagined.

Back at his desk, it seemed weird to Cole that she'd just been in his office. This woman that he'd thought at one point he was destined to only know from those morning jogs, then at another point never to see again, was now practically making herself a part of his life. He didn't have a problem with that.

"Cole." Chris knocked on the door frame. "Who was that woman?"

Cole was brought back to reality. "She's the journalist I told you about."

"The journalist?" Chris's eyes widened as he came into to the office. "The one you saw with Paul yesterday and outside of Sabrina's house?"

"Yes. The one we got the information on. She knows about alert.com."

"Damn!" Chris's hands clenched into fists. "What is she visiting you about?"

"I don't think she knows anything about you that would

matter to her." Cole sat at his desk, hands in pockets. "She has a file on us that Sabrina must've given her, but I don't think it's the documents. I don't think she has them."

"She has to. Sabrina had the documents, she has the file. Why did she give it to this woman?"

"Don't know yet, but it's not our papers. Maybe Sabrina gave the file to someone else."

"Paul?" Chris shook his head. "I think he's behind this. I don't like your idea of laying off him right now. You don't believe in coincidences any more than I do."

"Just trust me," Cole said. "I have him under surveillance, but if we push him, he might freak. If he's the key to this, we have to play it safe. Keep your enemies closer, right? Trust me, absolutely everything he is doing is being monitored."

"This Grant woman, too. Let's have her tailed."

Cole didn't like the thought of that. He already felt guilty about the information he had on her, how he'd gotten it. "I'm getting the file from her. It's all she has. Don't worry about Jesse. I'll handle her."

"How are you getting the file from her?"

"She's bringing it to me." Cole noticed the look of disbelief. "Look, trust, me okay? I have this under control. Just run your company and stop obsessing over this. I'm on it."

"I need to know what she has on me in that file."

"Why?" Cole asked. "What do you have to hide?"

"It's not what I have to hide. I don't want my personal information out there. Besides, what if she's getting wrong information from someone trying to sabotage my success?"

"This isn't about that, Chris. It's about alert.com."

"I know, but . . ." Chris was frustrated. "Just keep an

eye on Jesse Grant and Paul. Something bad is about to happen. I can feel it."

Cole was feeling it, too. Chris was acting as if he would lose it any second, which was not normal for him. Cole needed his boss to be cool right now, to run the company while he figured out where the documents were and how to protect alert.com before it was rolled out.

"I give up," Jesse growled as she clicked off her Internet connection. "There are literally no homes in Silicon Valley unless you make one million bucks."

"Quitter." Joan slid her chair into Jesse's cubicle. "There's something out there for you."

"There's a ton of homes perfect for me, but not my pocketbook. I guess I have to come up with some amazing software company and sell it for a gazillion dollars like everyone else here."

"Call a real estate agent."

"Leave me alone." Jesse returned to her work.

Joan laughed. "What's with your attitude?"

Jesse sighed. "I'm sorry. I'm just wound up. Cole Nicholson has got my brain going in circles."

"Tell me, Jesse. Would you prefer a challenge or a man who did whatever you say?"

"I could use a little of the latter," Jesse said. "And he will do what I say. It's just going to take some more maneuvering."

"Are you still mad you're giving him the file?"

"No. I just made a copy of everything for myself. No big deal. I just want more."

"Join the club. Don't we all?"

"I mean I want more information. Not just for the story,

but about that file. Those notes don't make much sense. It's like there's something missing. Something big, and it could be connected to Sabrina's death."

"So what is your master plan?"

"I'm going to look through the other files, and find . . ."

"Not with Sabrina. With Cole Nicholson. That's what I'm interested in."

"I don't know." Jesse's brows narrowed in frustration. "He's not as easy as I suspected he would be. Well, I guess I never thought he'd be easy. I just didn't figure I couldn't deal with him. He's like a brick wall almost."

"And you're not."

"I'm nothing like that. That's been my problem. I jump headfirst into everything and think about how wise it was afterward."

"I'm hearing Henry again."

"Stop it." Jesse knew she wasn't Henry-free yet. She didn't know if she ever would be. So what did that mean for her love life? It had just been so ugly and upsetting.

The phone rang and Jesse reached for it.

"Jesse Grant here."

"Jesse, this is Nina Flay with Branton Travel. I'm returning your phone call?"

"Oh, yes." Jesse shooed Joan away, but Joan wasn't budging. "I was calling about Sabrina Joseph. She was a friend of mine."

"I was so sorry to hear about her death. I can't believe she committed suicide."

"I'm not so certain she did, and I'm trying to prove that, but I need your help."

"Oh my goodness. I . . . murdered? Is that what you're saying?"

"Yes. I don't have any real proof of it. That's why I'm calling you.

"I didn't know her hardly at all. We worked on trips together probably twice a year."

"I just want to know about this most recent trip. When did she plan it?"

"She hadn't been planning it for that long. She called me a month or so ago with all these ideas about where she wanted to go. Anywhere warm. Caribbean, Hawaii, even Africa, which is Hades hot this time of year. I sent her everything I had and we talked for hours about each of the resorts."

"She seemed excited?"

"Yeah, from what I could tell. She couldn't make up her mind at first, but when we finally decided, she seemed more excited than I've seen anyone in a long time. She said it was going to be a rebirth."

Just what Jesse was looking for. "So she didn't seem depressed at all?"

"She was a little down when she said that some bad things had been happening to her lately. She didn't want to talk about them, but she was looking to start over. She kept saying it over and over again. She wanted a new life, had a new lover, and . . ."

"A new lover? Who?"

There was a pause. "I don't remember his name. She was excited about him. A distinguished executive type. He couldn't come with her on the trip, too busy working. From what she said, I'm thinking he was married. He never had enough time for her, and didn't seem too interested in going out when they were together. But she wanted to be on her own to focus on herself anyway. She said she needed to get away."

"But she wouldn't say from what."

"I guess those bad things I mentioned before that she didn't want to talk about. Oh, yeah. She said she was working on a couple of cases that were pretty dangerous. She's a P.I., you know."

"Yes, I do. What cases were those?"

"I can't remember everything she said. One was a man cheating on his wife with a model or actress. I think she almost got caught. There was another one, too. Basically she just said that for what she was making, it wasn't worth the risk she was taking, and it was getting on her nerves. She was going to be glad to leave it behind for a while."

"Thanks, Nina. You've helped me so much."

"I'm glad I could. Call me if I can be of any more help."

"I will." Jesse hung up.

"Tell me everything," Joan said immediately.

"No time for that, but Sabrina definitely did not kill herself."

"Looks like you got yourself a story, honey."

"I'm not looking for a story here. I'm looking for the truth, for justice."

"That's where you get the best stories. So you think this begins at Netstyles?"

"I'm not so sure." Jesse leaned back, her mind racing. "She had a lot of cases. That's a lot of suspects."

"Every case is probably juicy."

"I'm not looking for sensationalism." Jesse felt her adrenaline running. "I'm going to find out the truth about this. I need to attack those files."

"How do you plan on doing that? You do have a job already."

"I'll find time to make this happen."

"What about your other storyline? What about Cole Nicholson?"

"I'll handle him." Jesse knew she didn't sound convincing. She wasn't sure what she was going to do about him, but couldn't deny the excitement that figuring it out was giving her.

The Rosicrucian Egyptian Museum on Naglee Avenue in San Jose was a busy and vibrant tourist attraction. Architecturally inspired by the Egyptian Temple of Amon, the museum held the largest collection of Egyptian artifacts on exhibit in the western U.S. Even on a weekday, the building was full of people. It was the perfect place for someone to blend in doing something they shouldn't be.

Jesse noticed Dr. Robin Bryant as soon as he entered the museum. The picture Sabrina had taken of him and kept in his file folder was very clear. He was hard not to spot. The man looked like a GQ model. Tall, tanned, and very blond with Roman features and deep, dark blue eyes. He worked out, too—not buffed, but chiseled. He dressed in cool white slacks and a pale blue polo. A true Californian.

"Right on time, you cheating dog," she whispered to herself, pretending to read the newspaper when he looked her way.

It was noon on Wednesday. That was when Sabrina's notes said Dr. Bryant met with his mistress at the museum. Mrs. Bryant was looking for ammunition for her soon-to-be-filed divorce. Based on her conversation with Nina the travel agent, Jesse felt this was the best case with which to start. So here she was, waiting to get a look-see herself . . . trying to figure out why Sabrina thought the money wasn't worth it here. He didn't appear too nervous or suspicious. Maybe it was because he knew Sabrina was no longer a threat.

"Pay dirt," she said as the mistress entered.

She was obvious. Not just from the fact that she looked like your textbook Southern California supermodel, but the coy way she accidentally brushed against him. He pretended to cough and followed her down the hallway, about ten steps behind. With Jesse ten steps behind him.

It got a little tricky when they both made a bee-line for the Women of the Nile exhibit with a large sign over the door that read THIS EXHIBIT IS ON TOUR. DO NOT ENTER. Jesse leaned over the water fountain as the doctor looked behind him before going inside. Jesse took a deep breath and followed. Fortunately, the door slid open quietly, so no noise was made when she entered. She saw nothing at first. It was dark and messy. There were high crates and tall boxes stacked against themed backdrops that had been taken apart. Apparently while the exhibit was on the road, the room had become storage.

Jesse couldn't see either of them, but she heard them. Heard them clearly, and tiptoed toward the noise.

Jesse was shocked, even though she should have expected it. The noises hinted at it. The doctor and the model had their hands all over each other, blond hair flying about, hands groping, mouths devouring.

"Oh, Robin!" The model breathed her words out in between kisses. It was only for a second.

"Oh, Sarah!" His hand slipped up her thin tank top and grabbed roughly at her breast. "Oh, Sarah, it's been so long."

Jesse was in full view of them, but neither of them saw her. They were too engrossed in each other. Too engrossed to hear Jesse's feet shuffle as, suddenly, a hand grabbed her by the arm and pulled her back as another hand covered her mouth.

Jesse panicked as her body was lifted and carried. She was taken into a wall space that was filled only halfway. She was out of sight of the lovers. Someone swung her around, still keeping a hand on her mouth.

"Keep your mouth shut!" Cole whispered his warning, his face leaning into hers.

Jesse slapped his hand away, trying to get over the shock of seeing him. She spoke in an alarmed whisper. "What are you doing here?"

"What are *you* doing here?" Cole pushed her farther inside the wall space. There wasn't a lot of a room. They were practically on top of each other. "Who are those people?"

"How dare you follow me!" Jesse was fuming, realizing the irony in her words.

"Do you hear something?" Sarah's voice was labored and heavy, as if she'd run a marathon.

Cole quickly covered Jesse's mouth again, but she pulled his arm away by digging her nails into his skin. Her look dared him to try it again, and he didn't.

"No, Sarah," Dr. Bryant said. "Nothing but my heart."

"I thought I heard something. We're usually alone. The workers take a break from noon to one, don't they?"

"Let me look around."

Jesse felt her stomach tense as she heard footsteps. She held her breath. Cole didn't look at all scared, just annoyed. She wanted to kill him. She bit her lip as she heard the steps come right near the wall.

"Nobody's here, baby," the doctor said. "Now come here."

Within a second, the panting began again. Only this time, they were on the other side of the wall, only inches of plaster separating them from Jesse and Cole. They couldn't move. Jesse was panicked. Cole was right on her, their chests touching. She was too aware of his strength, his cologne. Despite being scared to death, Jesse was more distracted by his closeness than anything.

"Sarah, I miss you so much I can barely breathe," the doctor said.

"You sure it's okay we see each other again? I mean your wife, the private investigator she hired."

"I've handled my wife. She doesn't care who I'm with as long as she's secure. I made promises, and she's happy with our situation now. There's nothing to fear from a P.I. or anyone else. I just want to make love to you."

"Now?"

"Right now. Right here!"

Cole couldn't believe the situation he was in. Stuck in a wall space, this close to Jesse. Not too long ago, he had fantasized about being this close to her. Now that he was, its effect was stronger than he had expected. He was reacting to her proximity, and the moaning and panting only inches from them. Why did he have to pull her into a space barely big enough for one person? She was so beautiful, she smelled so good. Her arm, where his hands were still holding her, was so soft and tempting. He was praying this couple would stop with the passionate sounds.

Jesse could feel his breathing on her, his hands on her arms. She kept her eyes to his chest; watching it move up and down was strangely arousing to her. There was nowhere she could go. She could hear the lovers' hands groping each other, moving clothing out of the way, unbuttoning, lifting, unzipping. She could hear the smack of their lips as they kissed with abandon and could almost feel their heat through the wall.

Against her own will, as if her body ruled her, Jesse looked up at Cole. It was the last thing she wanted to do, because just as she thought, he was looking right at her. Their faces were so close, their eyes connecting as the lovers groaned in unison out loud. The thin wall between them moved with the couple. Jesse wanted to be disgusted, but she felt like she was on fire. She couldn't look away. His lips, his eyes . . .

This was unfamiliar territory for Cole. Not being close to a woman, but being so quickly overwhelmed by it. Cole didn't know what to do. He was about to lose control. Her full lips, an enticing shade of dark rose, were calling to him, her large eyes so uncertain, so afraid, seemed to be pleading for him. His hands on her arms were sweating now. He could feel one move slowly up her silky arm as if it had a mind of its own. Her eyes closed, and his other hand came to her neck, tilting her head slightly back.

"Oh, Robin!" Sarah screamed. "Oh God, Robin!"

Jesse's eyes closed by instinct. She could feel his arousal against her body, against her thin nylon purple summer dress. She moved her hip only an inch to the right, not knowing why. Her body wanted to. It was reacting to him, his closeness, and his hands and their effect on it.

Cole couldn't control it anymore. He had to kiss her, touch her more. Just as he lowered his face to hers, ready to do what he had wanted to for what seemed like forever, they were both jolted by a loud bang.

Jesse's eyes flew open. Sarah screamed and Dr. Bryant cursed a string of obscenities out loud. The security guard, barely visible to her, was in the room. He banged the wall with his flashlight, shining it indiscriminately about the room.

"Who's in here?" His voice was deep and bellowing.

"Officer." Dr. Bryant's voice was cracked and hoarse.

Jesse turned to Cole, who was staring directly at her. He put his index finger to his mouth in a gesture for silence. Jesse couldn't believe what had just happened, what had almost just happened. She looked away as she could hear the lovers hastily reapplying their clothes.

"What are you doing in here?" the security guard asked as he shone the flashlight on the lovers. "This is an off-limits area. No one is supposed to be in here. What in the hell are you two . . ."

"Nothing, officer." Dr. Bryant was approaching him now.

Sarah flew by them both, running out of the room with her head down in shame.

"I'm not an officer," the guy said. "You getting it on in here? Haven't you ever heard of a hotel room?"

"We're really sorry, sir." The doctor was still buttoning his shirt as he reached the door. "It's been weeks for us. It's been . . ."

"I don't care." The guard's voice sounded disgusted. "Get out of here. I should throw you out of the museum. There are kids running around here. If I catch you in an off-limits area again, you will be talking to an officer. And they won't let you walk away."

"Thank you, sir." The doctor almost bowed his head as he tucked his shirt halfway in and ran out the room.

Cole watched carefully, doing everything he could not to look at Jesse, as the guard flashed his light around the room. Seemingly satisfied, he flicked his flashlight off and left.

Jesse let out a deep breath as she slid away from Cole and out of the tiny space they had occupied. She still felt flushed, but was too proud to fan herself.

"Be quiet," Cole whispered, following her. "He could still be out there. He heard them. He could hear us."

"They were pretty loud," she said, surprised to hear her own voice. It was as cracked and breathy as the doctor's.

"Let me check." Cole avoided touching Jesse as he walked past her and headed for the door. He opened it slightly, peeking out. "He's gone. Let's go."

Jesse hesitated, not able to move at the moment.

He looked back at her and spoke in a more demanding voice. "Let's go, Jesse. Now."

She did as she was told, only because she didn't have a mind to protest his tone of voice with her. They left the exhibit area and were quickly immersed in the crowd. Jesse felt like everyone's eyes were on her, as if they knew that she had come so close to doing something she was certain she would regret.

Without even thinking of what he was doing, Cole grabbed her by the arm. "Come with me."

Jesse jerked away, a reaction so harsh and quick that it surprised even her. Right then, the thought of him touching her was too much. She was still reeling from her earlier reaction to their intimacy, to what had almost happened.

"I'm not a child. Don't grab me."

"Fine." Cole wasn't surprised by her reaction. What was going on between them was a little scary for him, too. But someone had to get serious. "Just come with me. We can talk in the museum cafeteria."

* * *

As they sat in the hectic, brightly lit cafeteria, neither Jesse nor Cole wanted to admit how caught up they had gotten in the intense moment earlier. Jesse was scared to death of what had happened, and Cole was angry with himself for his loss of control. He was angry for even being there.

"Fine," he said. "If you won't say anything then I'll get it going. You can start with what you were doing in that room with the couple in heat."

Jesse's eyes closed to slits as she threw him a hateful glance. How dare he! "No. I'd rather start with what you were doing in there."

"I'm following you," he said. "But I'm sure you figured that out."

"Why?" Jesse shuddered at the thought of all the times she'd turned around and Henry had been there following her. Anger began to take over. "Why would you do something like that? Don't you know how upsetting that can be to a person? Who do you think you are? How dare you violate my privacy?"

Cole was surprised by her sudden reaction. "Calm down, Jesse. I'm not stalking you."

Jesse stared at him, then rolled her eyes and looked away. If only he knew. "Then what were you doing?"

"I'm trying to find out what you're up to. I know you have Sabrina's file on Netstyles, and being a journalist, I suspected you would try to investigate. Am I right?"

"I actually have all of her files." Jesse wasn't even sure she should be telling Cole this, but something told her it was okay. He wasn't at all threatening to her. At least not to her safety. "Sabrina was working on several cases. I'm trying to find out which one of them might have led to her murder."

"Which explains . . . "

"That couple was an extramarital affair Sabrina was spying on. Her travel agent said she had mentioned there were risks involved in this case and another case that Sabrina didn't think were worth taking."

"I don't doubt it," Cole said, optimistic that the murder could be related to other things. "What was the other one?"

"She couldn't remember. I'm going through all of them."

Okay, Jesse said to herself, *we're going to completely ignore that we came close to the same place where those illicit lovers were just minutes ago. Fine.*

"What brought you to her travel agent?" Cole figured if they kept talking, if he kept thinking, he would forget about what had just happened between them. He hoped so.

"Sabrina had made travel plans just a week before she died. She was planning on going to the Caribbean next week. Proof positive that she didn't commit suicide."

"Not proof positive," he said. "You have a tendency to state individual speculation as fact."

"I do not." Jesse glared at him again. "Are you still trying to act like you doubt this?"

"Fine, Jesse." He found even her obstinate stares attractive. "I believe she was murdered, okay? That's the reason why I'm following you."

"There's something besides Netstyles that actually interests you?"

"Very funny." Her comments did stab at him a little, because the answer to that question really was no, and he was a grounded enough man to know that was nothing to be proud of. "Because I have to take back some of what I said to you in my office."

"Don't you dare try to weasel out of our deal." Jesse was pointing a threatening finger in his face. "You promised."

"Not that." He didn't doubt for a second that she would have her retribution if he failed to pull his end of the deal. "What I told you about my boss, Chris Spall. I'm not sure he's as squeaky-clean as I thought."

Jesse could see the expression on his face turn somber. This was hard for him to admit. She felt sorry for him. "You respect him a lot."

"He's a technology genius and a great businessman. He's been a key part of my growth in the last three years. He's got a family that loves him, and he provides for them very well. I want to be like that one day. I want people to respect me for more than my ability to run a company."

Jesse felt her heart tug. Was she really sitting across from a gorgeous, wealthy man who dreamt of having a family and providing for them? She blinked to see if she was dreaming.

"I'm starting to feel some doubts," he continued, "even though I think they're unfounded. I just know that if I find out what really happened to her, I'll feel at ease."

"Because you're sure it won't lead to Chris?"

Cole paused and sighed. "It can't. Chris has his faults. He's not perfect, but he's not a killer. He can't be."

"But let's just speculate," Jesse said. "If so, why would he want to kill her?"

"I won't speculate," Cole said, "because he wouldn't. But I think someone was trying to get something on him. I'm not sure why. He's not sure why. But Netstyles's success has garnered a lot of jealousy. Probably more of that than admiration. Alert.com is what's most important to him right now, and we think that's what they want to use against him. Cheat him out of the chance to make a success out of it, or use it for extortion. But what they might not know is that they're really cheating me. Alert.com is mine."

"What is it?" Jesse saw him hesitate. "Come on. Do you think I'm the enemy?"

"You're the press, and I can't afford to let this get out to the public." Cole felt an unusual urge to share his secrets with her. It was her. There was something about her that made him want to do the opposite of what he knew he should. "If a competitor were to catch on, there would be a challenge to our product before we had a chance to dominate the market."

"Off the record, then." Jesse was excited to learn what was at the center of his life, and wouldn't give up easily.

Cole eyed her sternly. He knew she would never tell anyone. She was a trustworthy person. The honesty in her eyes told him so.

"Alert.com is a software product." Cole looked around, feeling self-conscious every time he talked about it. No one was thinking about either of them, but he was so entrenched in the secrecy of it, he couldn't help himself. "I created it to help the Internet user to be kept abreast of anything they'd want."

"Like what?"

"The weather, their stocks, whatever type of breaking news they'd like, whether it be consumer-related, entertainment, or political. Alert.com surfs the Net and delivers the latest to you. The key is, it will let you know it's got news for you, even if you aren't on the Internet. You can connect it to your cell phone, your television, anything digital."

"Cool," was all Jesse could say. But from the look on

Cole's face, that was enough. He was as proud as a new father, and his expression warmed her to him.

"Very cool." Cole appreciated her enthusiasm. "You see, it doesn't have to be any particular site you request, because there are a billion sites out there, and thousands being added every day. You don't have the time to search them all, find out if they have something you'd be interested in. With alert.com, you don't have to."

"You mean I can tell it that I want to know everything there is on eye shadow and it will send it to me from any Web site?"

"Every Web site that has even a sentence on eye shadow. You can make it more specific that that. You can say a particular brand of shadow, a color. It sends you whatever it finds as it searches the Web for you. It's different from a search engine, because it doesn't need any prompting from you. No more eighty-six percent match for giving you what you want one hundred percent. If you want to know about canoes in India, you'll only get information on canoes in India. Not canoe shops in Indiana. Let's say you like Michelangelo. If . . ."

"I love Michelangelo," Jesse offered. "He's my favorite artist."

"Okay," he continued, laughing at her enthusiasm. "So you tell alert.com you want to hear what's new about Michelangelo."

"New? He's been dead forever."

"Yes, but a museum in Colorado is having a special exhibit on him. A cruise to Italy is offering a special tour of his structures and paintings. A new course on his life or his art is being offered at Harvard University. As soon as that news hits the Web, alert.com sends it to you."

Jesse racked her brain. "There's nothing like that on

the market now. It would save so much time. It would be incredible."

"Very incredible." Cole felt a wave of attraction come over him at the delight in her eyes.

There was a silence as they both sensed the anxiety lessen between them. They were having a good time together, and that didn't make either of them feel particularly comfortable.

"I don't like being followed," Jesse said seriously. "I know you don't mean it personally, but I have a problem with that."

"I won't follow you anymore." Cole could tell she meant it. There was something more to it than the irritation. "I'll come along with you."

"I beg your pardon?"

"You're going to check out each of Sabrina's cases to find out which ones might have a connection to her death? I'll come along. I want to find out the same thing. I want to be able to get rid of these questions I have about Chris. It's important to the success of Netstyles and our relationship."

"What's in it for me?" Jesse asked, not certain she could handle being in another precarious situation with Cole anytime soon. She preferred to keep him out in the open, like in a museum cafeteria flowing with tourists.

Cole thought about it. "How about a chance to mingle with over one hundred African-American technical engineers and Internet company professionals in the Silicon Valley over chicken piccata?"

"How about it?" Jesse's eyes lit up.

"Would you like it or not? It would help you with your story."

"Of course I would." She socked him in the arm. He

was harder than she expected, bringing back memories of his muscles glistening in the sun as he passed her on the beach.

"Fine. Then you can be my guest at the Black Engineers of Silicon Valley Association summer dinner. It's Friday night at seven sharp. Semiformal."

"Where?"

Cole waited for her to get out a pen and paper. "1519 Dudvon Court, Mountain View."

"Snazzy." Jesse knew that was a high-rent area. "How am I getting in? Don't I need an invite to these things?"

"You'll be my date."

Jesse ignored the twirl in her stomach she felt at the thought, but it couldn't be that simple. Nothing ever was. "You mean to tell me the dashing Mr. Nicholson doesn't have a date only two days before the event? You must have a girlfriend or someone special."

Jesse wasn't sure she wanted the answer to that. Something inside her warned her that she would be greatly disappointed if he did have a someone special.

"She's in New York." Cole caught himself, but it was too late. He'd wanted to say no, but that would be a lie and that wasn't fair to Tracy or to Jesse. Why should it matter anyway? The last thing he needed was the attention of another woman. Even the one whose attention he wanted the most. Besides, technically, Tracy was still his girlfriend, and she would be until he had the guts to do something about it.

"Oh." Jesse knew if she waited too long to say anything it would be obvious that she was disappointed. Her heart was yelling out, *But what about all those smiles, those glances at the beach, that look you gave me across the street? The look you were giving just a moment ago?*

Cole felt awkward. "So, well . . . it's a deal then. We have an agreement?"

Jesse nodded. She just wanted to leave now. She had no interest in this banter any longer. "I have to get back to work at the office. I can't talk anymore."

"Wait!" Cole called out. "Our interview. Did you . . ."

"Monday," Jesse said as she slid out of her seat. "Your secretary said Monday at two was the earliest."

"I'm sorry," he said, apologizing for so much more than a delayed appointment. "It's been so . . ."

"I know." Jesse stood up. "We're all busy."

Cole was disappointed as she grabbed her purse. He wanted her to stay, but didn't. It was confusing, hard to explain. Part of him was so happy to be sitting across from her talking to her so freely. Just knowing her name brought him joy. The other part of him wanted to go back to the glances and smiles on the beach. At least then, she didn't interfere with his work, his life. She had just brought him joy for five seconds a day. And that had been enough for a long time.

"What about the file?" he called after her. Anything to keep her near for a moment longer.

"I'll bring it to the dinner tomorrow night. I'll meet you there at seven, right?"

"I'll be waiting for you. We'll talk about getting together for the other cases tomorrow night, too, right?"

Jesse paused, noticing the excitement had left his face as well. Had she just imagined that he was enjoying her company? Maybe she was. The romantic in her made her such a fool.

Jesse didn't want to look back, because if he wasn't looking at her, it would hurt her. If he was, it would scare her.

Hurt her because she wanted to believe he felt something. Scare her, because if he did, she wouldn't know what to do about it.

"Damn you, Henry," she said to herself. "I've let you make me an emotional chicken. Exactly what you wanted."

Chapter Five

"Don't tell me you aren't trying to impress him," Joan said. "Not with that outfit."

Jesse turned away from her, her head held high. "I'm not trying to impress him, Joan. I'm trying to impress all the people he's going to introduce me to."

Jesse knew she was lying. And as she looked at herself in her hallway mirror, she knew what this was about. She looked striking in an eggplant purple sheath-styled silk dress. The spaghetti straps exposed her shining dark skin, well-rounded shoulders, and long arms. The royal dip across the chest flattered her figure. The dress tapered at the waist, accentuating her flat stomach, the feature she loved the most. Then it flowed with femininity down to her ankles, with a tasteful slit up the left side. Her sequined black pumps were the finishing touch.

"Cole is the furthest thing from my mind." She ran a comb over her hair one last time. It was glossy and waved back. She wasn't fooling anybody. She looked good, and despite her better judgment, she wanted Cole to notice.

"Yeah, and I'm on the cover of next month's *Essence* magazine. Didn't I tell you? I'll get you your free copies tomorrow. I . . ."

"Oh, stop." Jesse headed for her living room, knowing Joan was right behind her. The moment she'd told her about the dinner, Joan hadn't left her alone for a second. She'd shown up, without warning as usual, claiming to be there to help her get ready. As if this were a date. It wasn't a date.

"But you're attracted to him," she said. "You know you are. I made some calls and found out that's he's a prime piece of meat for the market."

"What would Ray think if he heard you now?" Jesse took a deep breath. Her stomach was tied up in knots.

"The man is a gorgeous, black millionaire who is available and heterosexual." Joan laughed. "Ray couldn't blame me."

Jesse turned to her, beyond the point of pretense. "Available? Who told you that? He told me he has a girlfriend."

"I thought it didn't matter." Joan sighed, reaching for a magazine, but Jesse ripped it out of her hand.

"Talk to me, girl," she ordered.

"Her name is Tracy Neal." Joan smiled at the eager expression on Jesse's face. "Don't ask me how I know. I'll just tell you I got all this legit. Anyway, she's a business executive, and she's in New York."

"He told me that." Jesse didn't care to rehash what she knew. It only brought thoughts of their encounter in the museum and that made her too uncomfortable.

"My source says that they barely even speak to each other. As a matter of fact, she said she has a source in New York that tells her that Tracy has been creeping."

"Hmm." Jesse shrugged her shoulders. "Whatever she's up to, it doesn't matter to me. This is a professional relationship. I need him for my story series and to find out about Sabrina. That's it."

"That's for the better," Joan said.

"What do you mean by that?"

Joan took a long sip of the wine cooler she had left on the table. She sat on the sofa, leaning back. "Well, I don't trust him. Personally, from what you've told me about Sabrina's investigation, I wouldn't want to be alone in a room with him."

"If he was dangerous, why would he try and help me?" Jesse said. "Why would he want to find out what was going on with Sabrina's other cases if he didn't care?"

"To divert you, girlfriend. He's trying to help you to make you think that he's a good guy, and he wants to follow you on these cases, so that he can make sure you're focusing on something other than him. The real suspect."

"You're ridiculous. Cole wasn't Sabrina's target. Chris was. And he wants to find out the truth, because he believes Chris is innocent. If he was guilty, he wouldn't want to prove Chris innocent, because then he would be the first alternative suspect. You should've seen the look on his face when he talked about Chris. He really admires the guy."

Joan looked at her suspiciously. She took another long sip.

"What?" Jesse asked, not liking that look at all.

"Professional relationship, my ass," she said. "You sound like a woman defending your man."

Jesse clenched her fists. "Are you trying to play another

game with me? One of those make-Jesse-step-on-her-own-tongue-so-she-can-realize-everything-ends-up-being-about-Henry games?"

"No. But since you brought it up."

"Nothing about this has to do with Henry and his freaking psycho behavior. He's in jail now. He'll be there for a long time. There's no reason for me to be afraid. He can't hurt me."

"But another man could. That's what you're thinking, and that's what I'm trying to get at. You were pretty damaged by what Henry did to you, so yeah, you had six months to deal with it. But it's time you start dating again, and you simply refuse. You're afraid you'll get another Henry."

"I'm fine with my life right now." Jesse didn't want Joan dampening her mood. "I don't need a man in it to complicate things. And who's to say I wouldn't get another Henry? It's not like I could see when I met him that he was Jekyll and Hyde."

"You know what?" Joan asked as she got off the sofa. "You gotta get back to trusting yourself. You take too long, you could miss out on the guy that could make you forget all about Henry."

Jesse sighed, pretending to be bored with the conversation. "Leaving then?"

"Yes." Joan stuck her tongue out. "You have fun tonight. Professionally, I mean."

"Of course."

Jesse took one last glance at herself in the mirror once Joan left. She couldn't stop thinking of Cole, but images of Henry worked their way into her mind. She closed her eyes tightly and clenched her fists.

"Get the hell out of my life, Henry."

Opening her eyes, she slid her hands down the sides of her dress, skimming her hips, and headed out the door.

Jesse was impressed. The house at Dudvon Court was imposing, as were most Mountain View homes. Tech millionaires retreated to the mountainous paradise to escape the city. Only they could afford to live there.

This house was made of dark gray stone. It was two floors, going up high with a chimney in the back on the left side. The outside was lined with small trees and pines. The large, winding driveway was red brick, wrapping around the house, possibly to a garage around the side that couldn't be seen, and lining a large front yard filled with luxury cars. The front door reached all the way to the second floor, with a half circle arch at the top.

As Jesse's car approached the driveway, the valet jumped to open the door for her. Very impressed, she got out of the car and looked around. There was no one out front, just a bunch of cars. No Cole. She checked her watch. It was seven on the dot.

As the valet drove away, Jesse made her way to the front door and decided to wait a little longer. She didn't need Cole to go in. She'd gone to too many places uninvited to let that bother her. It was only that she wanted these people to like her, to let her interview them. She wasn't doing much for her cause by crashing their party.

"He better not be much later," she said to herself.

The valet who parked her car gave her a quizzical look as he returned to the driveway. Jesse was beginning to feel stupid. She got nervous when he began to approach her.

She was relieved when a van pulled up and he turned to attend to it. A man with a violin stepped out and talked to the valet, who then pointed to the side of the house. The violinist went that way, and the valet took the van.

The second time he returned, he headed straight for Jesse. She was tempted to turn and walk in before he could talk to her, but he called out to her just as she turned. She had to turn back.

"Yes?" she asked.

"Can I help you with something?" he asked. "You know you don't have to wait out here. Even though it's a wonderful night. You can go right in."

"I'm waiting for someone," she said, at least relieved that he wasn't trying to get rid of her.

The valet laughed. He was, in a word, a nondescript type of person. Not one to be noticed often. "That's good. I was afraid you were waiting for me to get the door for you. Mr. Nicholson would kill me if someone came and complained to him."

"Cole Nicholson?"

"Yeah. There was supposed to be a guy getting the door, but he couldn't make it. So it's just me."

"So Cole has already arrived? You've spoken to him?"

He looked at her funny, confused. "What do you mean, arrived? Of course he has. It's his house."

Jesse's surprise turned to anger. Without a word, she turned and stormed into the house. The house was relatively empty, with just a few people standing around, most of them in catering outfits. It was brightly lit and well decorated in neutral colors and pinewood. Jesse asked a short, broad woman with a plate of tiny quiches where Cole was. She was directed to the kitchen.

There he was. The second Jesse entered the kitchen, she was hit with contradicting emotions. She wanted to curse him out, but he looked . . . he looked so good. In his casual evening suit, the fabric hung like it was made for him; made for the contours of his body. It was a body treated with care. Jesse had never seen a man so comfortable in his own skin. It was such an appealing quality. She wanted to smack herself for being so attracted to him.

"How dare you!" she said, forcing herself to get back on track.

Cole turned away from the head caterer. A smile lit his face when he saw her. She was absolutely breathtaking in a dress that dared you not to stare at her. He felt a breeze hit his face that could only be her. He sensed the tension inside him, in the pit of his stomach. He noticed the look on her face and halted.

"How dare I what?" He walked toward her, wanting to touch her again.

"How long were you planning on letting me stand outside?" Jesse noticed how he'd looked at her, noticed how it made her feel. *Concentrate,* she told herself. *You're mad at him, remember?* "An hour? Was that supposed to be a joke?"

"What are you talking about? You were waiting outside? Why?"

"We agreed to meet here at seven, you jerk. You knew I would be waiting outside."

"I don't remember saying anything about outside." He tried to control his laughter. She looked as if she could slap him right then. He kept his distance.

"That's standard practice, Cole. You know that. When you agree to meet someone for a date, you meet outside. You knew I . . ."

"A date?" His lips formed a smile. "This is a date?"

"Of course not." She frowned at him. "This is a business deal. Nothing like a . . ."

"You said date."

"No, I didn't." Jesse sighed in annoyance. "This is nothing like a date."

Cole lifted a finger. "You specifically said, 'When you agree to meet someone for a *date*, you meet outside.' "

"I didn't say that. Stop toying with me." Jesse pressed her lips together.

"I'm not." God, how he liked her spirit.

"I said, 'When you agree to meet someone, you meet outside'."

"That's not what you said. You said . . ."

Jesse's hands were on her hips. "How are you gonna try and tell me what I said?"

"Woman." Cole's eyes squinted tightly, sharply. "Look, we'll get nowhere with this. I'm sorry, okay. I'm sorry I made you think I would meet you outside. For our date."

"Shut up." Jesse pouted. "I have half a mind to hand this file over to you and leave."

"That only hurts you." Cole knew he was lying. He very much wanted her to stay. Very much.

"Which is why I'm not leaving." She handed him the file. "That would fall perfectly into your plan. I expect to leave here on a first-name basis with everyone."

"I'll do my best." He took her by the arm. "Come with me."

Jesse felt a spark the second he touched her. Generally, she resisted any man taking her by the arm. She found it a sexist movement. But in this case, she liked it. She liked it a lot and said nothing as he led her down the hallway. He stopped a moment to drop the file in a mysterious room with a closed door. Jesse took a peek inside, but it was dark and Cole only opened the door wide enough to slide in and out, and then closed it behind him.

"Shall we get started?" he asked.

Jesse shrugged. "This better be good."

He turned to her, noticing that sarcastic grin on her lips. She liked having the last word.

It was good. As they entered Cole's backyard, the lights and music hit Jesse with that familiar feeling. The feeling of a good time. The sun was setting, and there were tiki torches placed generously around the very large yard lined with a short stone fence. There was a buffet table of all types of food in splendid, vibrant colors, and small round tables, almost blindingly white, all over the place. There were at least one hundred people sitting at them or standing around them in conversation.

Jesse felt a strong sense of belonging and comfort with Cole's hand at her back as he introduced her to person after person. With such charisma and charm, Jesse realized he was nothing like the average techie—all circuits and chips, and no personality. Cole was the full package, and everyone there that night knew so. The way they reacted to him, with respect and admiration, made him all the more appealing to Jesse. It was difficult, but she tried hard to concentrate on the matter at hand: subjects for her story series.

Anthony Conrad was a senior software engineer for the leading computer company in all of Silicon Valley. Lita Quinn ran public relations for a new telecommunications company with ties to the Internet. Julia Charles was a product manager for a cellular phone company. Her newest product helped customers access their E-mail from their cellular phones. Bill Castle and Brendan Astin were CEOs and founders of an Internet site devoted to social and professional networking for African American professionals worldwide. An Internet First Fridays. Miles Doyle was a young software engineer, hired by Cole on a campus recruiting visit to Howard University. They all agreed to meet with Jesse, promising to have enough information for her to bring this issue back to life. But still, with all of this, it was Cole's arm, a constant against her back, that Jesse was most aware of. How it made her feel safe, comforted. She wasn't sure a man could make her feel that way again.

Cole was filled with mixed emotions during the evening. He felt guilty because he hadn't connected with these people in a long time. He knew many of them saw him as a leader in the organization because of his status in the industry. These were men and women who had been a source of support since his Stanford days.

He was also having a good ol' time seeing old friends, sharing his home. Good food, a great evening. It reminded him of better, less stressful days.

Then there was Jesse. The effect she was having on him. She was becoming a part of his life just like that. As much as he had thought he wanted that when he had seen her at the beach, the realization was surreal to him. She was so beautiful, charming, and intelligent. She showed such a yearning for what she was writing about that it inspired everyone she talked to. Everyone took to her immediately, and he had begun to feel such a sense of pride that she was there because of him . . . in a way, with him.

It probably wasn't wise, but he was letting himself get used to her, and it only made him want to know her even better.

Everyone had eaten, and turned their attention to dancing, drinking, and mingling. Jesse wasn't sure at what point she had lost Cole. He had given a quick speech while everyone was seated and somehow never made it back to the table. As the night went on, Jesse had warmed to Dean James, Cole's best friend. He was definitely more of a free spirit than the generally conservative crowd. More like her.

"So you appear to be the woman of the hour," Dean said as he led Jesse to the dance floor.

"You're flattering me," she said with a modest smile. "I would say Cole was the man of the hour. He's a master at hosting a party."

"Yeah, but it's got to be because of you."

"That's silly." Jesse shook her head. "Why would it be me?"

"I haven't seen Cole be this social in almost a year. The only thing different in his life is you."

"I'm not in his life. He's helping me, I'm helping him. It's a business arrangement."

"Whatever you want to call it, it's what has him *en fuego* tonight. Which, in turn, makes you the woman of the hour, as I said before. Thanks for bringing him back to us."

"Where has he been?"

"He'd kill me if I said anything. I couldn't . . ."

"Alert.com?" Jesse noticed Dean's look of surprise. "It's found its way into our business arrangement."

"You probably know more about it than me."

Jesse was surprised. "He said you were his best friend. You don't know about it either?"

"No, and I am his best friend. That's how important this is to him. We used to share everything. No secrets. He used to do stuff like this all the time."

"Host parties?"

Dean laughed. "Well, not this exactly. To tell you the truth, this is about the nicest event we've ever had. This party was invitation only. It was one hundred bucks a person."

"To cover costs?" Jesse looked around. "Was it that expensive?"

"No. The money goes toward Silicon City."

"Silicon City?"

"It's a project Cole started five years ago. It takes Silicon Valley to the inner cities. Hence the name. Poor areas, and yes, there are poor areas in Silicon Valley. He uses Silicon City to get computers in their libraries, public housing centers, and community centers so the residents can have computers, access to the Internet, CD-Rom learning games, and stuff like that."

"Wow." Jesse looked around for Cole. Where was he? She wanted to see him, tell him that maybe she had him wrong. "I thought . . . I thought he didn't really care about this stuff. You know, activism, social issues."

"He cares, but he hasn't done much of anything in the past year. He's given up everything—charity, friendships, relationships, everything—for this product. I can't even believe he told you what it was called. Did he tell you what it does?"

Jesse feigned zipping her lips. "I couldn't tell you. I might end up missing. He's very protective of this thing."

"I'm afraid to think of how protective."

Jesse found that an awkward statement. "What do you mean by that?"

She noticed a sudden discomfort take over Dean's face. He looked away for a moment.

"Cole is your best friend," she said. "I don't expect you to say anything about him. I'm concerned about Chris Spall."

"What do you know, Jesse Grant?"

"Nothing really. I know Sabrina Joseph. I knew her. How about you?"

"You're going to have to talk to Cole about her. I can't get involved in this stuff. My history is sensitive to foul play."

"Is that so?" Jesse let the topic go for now. She'd get more from Cole. If she could find him.

"One dance is enough."

Jesse turned around to see Tanya James, Dean's wife, standing behind them.

"I trust my husband and all," she said as she wrapped her arms around him, smiling at Jesse. "But you're a little too cute for more than one dance. And he's a little too charming."

"He's all yours again." Jesse smiled as she relinquished her dancing partner. She had someone else on her mind anyway.

Jesse returned to the house in search of Cole. The rooms were large, and the hallway was enormous. The decorating style was typical of urban professionals who were living in means at such a young age. Clean and neat, with a hint of personal style, but not very thought out. Twenty-first-century tech money.

"Where are you, Cole Nicholson?" Jesse stood in the hallway looking around. He wasn't in the kitchen, the living room, the foyer. Maybe he was up . . .

Jesse smiled, remembering. The file. She made her way to the study and slowly opened the door. Cole looked up to face her, the file open in his hands. He was leaning against the front of the desk. He looked so cool and collected, so casually masculine, all alone and silent.

"So there you are." Jesse closed the door behind her and slowly, flirtatiously walked toward him. The look on his face as he saw her told her that he was pleased. That he wouldn't ask her to leave.

"Here I am." He closed the file, happy to see her. He had been very eager to get back to her, but work had called. "You enjoying yourself?"

"Tremendously. This party is a gold mine. Thanks for bringing me."

"We made a deal. Besides, it was my pleasure." She had no idea how much it was his pleasure. The silence of the room, absence of a crowd, and the dim light next to them created a sensual essence around her.

Jesse smoothed her dress out. She was enjoying the way he was looking at her too much. A voice in the back of her head asked her what she thought she was doing. Thinking this way had gotten her in trouble too many times. "If it was such a pleasure, why did you leave me?"

"I wanted to take a look at this file." Cole noticed how her hips and body moved. How her hands coasted down her dress.

"Is it what you expected?" She wondered if she should tell him that she had made a copy of it all for herself. No. She was sure he suspected that much.

He placed the file on the desk and folded his arms across his chest. His shirt had come a little undone, but Jesse thought it only made him sexier, with a rugged edge to the refined style.

"No." Cole couldn't hide his disappointment. "You were right. These are just notes of her spying on Chris. It doesn't even really say why. At least not where I can read it."

Jesse leaned against the desk next to him. "Penmanship was definitely not one of Sabrina's strong points. So what's next?"

Cole smiled. The smell of her perfume returned to his senses. He smiled wider. "I'm looking for documents from our company. They were stolen from us the same night that Sabrina posed as a member of the night cleaning crew."

"Sabrina an infiltrator?" Jesse shook her head. "She is certainly a surprise. I wouldn't figure she had it in her."

"The video cameras say she does. Did."

There was a silence as they both realized they were talking about a dead woman.

"So what are you going to do?" Jesse asked. She could see he was upset. She wanted to console him, felt almost compelled to, but she held back.

"Keep looking. I have to find out what she did with them." He clenched his hands into fists. "Jesse, I just don't know what I'll do if someone tries to steal this from me."

"You sound like your life depends on it."

"I've sacrificed so much." He shook his head. "I'm not acting as if I've suffered or anything like that. But I've put my heart and soul into this product. I've set everything else aside. And I do mean everything."

"Like Silicon City?"

He looked at her. "How do you . . . yes, even that. I want alert.com to be my mark."

"I would think you would want Silicon City to be your mark. You could take it national, global. It's more lasting, more affecting. Internet products don't last forever."

He nodded. "But charity doesn't move money in the business world. Products do. Bottom lines."

"You have that. You're going to be CEO."

"I need alert.com to come out before that. You know, there is a downside to all this publicity about minorities in the tech industry, although ninety-five percent of it is positive."

"The public has to know about a problem before they

can take a stand against it or for it," Jesse said. "You believe in that, don't you? I mean, more than racism, ignorance hurts our people."

"You're right." He felt good about Jesse. She had a good heart. It was in the right place. A woman like her could keep him on the straight and narrow. "But there's that other five percent. You see, when it's so public like this, when a company does take action, everyone . . . well, a lot of people at least, will believe it's because they fear repercussions, want to look good. Anything but because it's what they were going to do anyway. Chris is leaving soon, and I'm going to take over Netstyles. Alert.com is what's going to shut up anyone who tries to say my appointment to CEO is because Chris wanted to show a little support for the colored-folks situation on his way out."

It took all of Jesse's strength to keep from wrapping her arms around him. "But Cole, you have a reputation already. I've read about you. I've listened to what everyone here tonight has to say about you."

"That doesn't mean anything to people out there. To them, I'm still a . . ." He sighed. "Look at me. I'm complaining, feeling sorry for myself. I vowed that I would never let the discrimination I faced in the business world make me bitter and self-defeating."

"Do you know the difference between complaining and expressing what's in your heart?" Jesse asked, sliding closer to him. *What are you doing girl? You are going way too fast.*

"What's the difference?" Her closeness caused a physical, chemical reaction inside of Cole. He had such a thing for this woman.

"The person listening," she said. "If they care about you, it's never complaining."

Their eyes connected and the room disappeared. Jesse

felt a rush run through her. Cole felt a fire ignite in him. They both knew what was coming next.

Cole's hand reached for Jesse's hair, tapering at the back of her neck. Her arms wrapped around his back as his lips came down to hers. They both turned sideways as their bodies joined.

The touch of his lips on her sent Jesse ablaze. The kiss was demanding and hungry and her body's response was immediate. She kissed him back, digging her fingers into his back.

Cole felt an animal hunger start in his groin and spread throughout his body. His hand gently held her head, while the other went to her waist. The material of her dress could not contain the heat he felt from her body. His lips pressed against hers, wanting more. His breathing was out of control. He heard a moan escape Jesse, and his tongue entered her mouth. This time the moan was his as the taste of her was sweet and warm, throwing his world out of order.

Jesse was riding waves of ecstasy as his tongue explored her mouth, hers doing the same with his. Her body moved with passion as Cole began to pull her dress up.

"Damn, Jesse." His voice was barely audible, even though he was speaking into her ear.

Jesse's mouth found his again, and reclaimed it, her hands pulling his head to her. She wanted his lips more than she had ever wanted anything. As she felt his hands move up the inside of her thighs, her stomach ached.

Frantically, she grabbed at the buttons of his shirt, separating her mouth from his only a moment to find them.

As she unbuttoned his first button, then the second, Cole wasn't sure he could wait much longer. He reached behind her and slid his hand over his desk, forcing everything on top of it to the floor.

"Oh, Cole," Jesse called out as he lifted her body up again and laid her on the desk. The idea of what was going to happen, especially where, was so exciting to her that she tore at his shirt, letting the rest of the buttons go flying. As he positioned himself on top of her, her dress was above her waist, revealing silky white panties. She saw the desire in his eyes as he reached for them, his finger . . .

"Oh my god!"

Cole and Jesse both jumped up, the yell of an intruder and the bright lights coming on suddenly jolting the rest of the world back into their consciousness. Cole quickly got up and off the desk, trying to regain his composure. Jesse took a little longer, still dazed by the entire event. She swung around and got off the table with her back to Cole and the interrupting party. She felt light-headed and dizzy, but quickly pulled her dress back down, smoothing it out.

"What is it?" Cole's voice was broken, hoarse, his breathing heavy. He began buttoning his shirt back, but realized most of the buttons were gone and gave up.

"I'm really sorry," the young woman said with an eastern European accent. The look on her face was pure horror and embarrassment. So much so that she couldn't leave if she wanted to. "Mr. Nicholson, I . . ."

"I've asked you . . . not to . . . call me that," he said in anger. He looked back at Jesse. Seeing her back to him angered him for some reason. "What do you want?"

"It's the phone. There's a call for you."

Cole ran a hand down his face, trying to gain control again. He took a deep breath. God, he was hot. "I told you I didn't want any calls unless it was an emergency."

Jesse tried to search through her feelings. She recognized the obvious ones, but the fear was a surprise to her.

How she had lost control. She was about to have sex with a man she barely knew on top of a desk in a room with a crowd of strangers right outside! Why was she so reckless when it came to this kind of thing? Hadn't she learned her lesson?

"Well, yes, sir. But, it's Ms. Neal."

Tracy! Jesse's eyes flew open, and she felt suddenly sick to her stomach. She had forgotten all about Tracy. Cole had a woman! Now she was turning into a man stealer?

Cole felt guilt wash over him. He knew he should not have done what he did, but . . . everything within him told him that it was right. What was happening to him? He wasn't a cheater. He looked back at Jesse. Her back was still to him. She didn't know Tracy was his girlfriend.

Suddenly she turned around to face him. The look on her face told him that somehow she did know who Tracy was, and she hated him for it. What had he done?

"Sir?" The woman's eyes shifted from Cole to Jesse. She seemed scared out of her wits. "Ms. Neal. What should I tell her?"

"Take the call, Cole," Jesse said, trying her best to appear in control. Her mind was still whirling, her gut reacting to his touch, his kiss, his body. Her anger and guilt forced her pride to hold its course. "Can't keep your girlfriend waiting."

"Leave," was all Cole said to the woman, who ran out quickly. "Jesse, I . . ."

"Please don't." Jesse held up her hand to stop him. She couldn't even look at him. Her eyes turned away, to the desk. The bare desk upon which their bodies had just been about to do all sort of unmentionables. "I've got to get out of here."

"Don't go, Jesse." Cole grabbed her arm as she passed

him. He didn't want her to go, to hate him. "I can explain Tracy."

"There's no need to explain," she said, ripping his hand away. Just the touch of him made her see stars. "Tracy is your girlfriend. That's enough explanation for me. This is ridiculous. I don't know how this happened."

"It was my fault, Jesse. I shouldn't have . . ."

"Don't be a gentleman right now, Cole. I don't think I could take that. This shouldn't have happened period. We can both share the blame and let it be at that."

"Let it be?" Cole stepped closer to her. "Jesse, I don't want . . ."

"What you want doesn't matter." Jesse stepped away. "At least not to me. That's Tracy's territory. Take your call, Cole. I'm leaving. And I want this to stay professional, what we're doing. We made a deal. It didn't include playing house on the desk."

"That was more than playing house," Cole said. Much more. "I think we should talk about it at least."

"What's to talk about?" she asked with a sarcastic laugh. "Actions speak louder than words, right? Look, whatever that was, it wasn't part of the deal. So let's make sure it doesn't happen again."

"I'm sorry, Jesse." Cole wanted to argue that point, but he knew he had no right to. He had no right to anything he was feeling right now. "It won't happen again."

Jesse had already turned her back to him and was quickly out the door. After she left the room, she sprinted outside the house.

"Are you okay?" The valet asked as she asked for her car. "You look upset."

Jesse laughed, feeling like she wanted to cry. "I'm just fine. As always. Just fine. My life makes total sense. Can you get my car, please? I have got to get away from here as soon as possible."

"Yes, ma'am."

Jesse touched her fingers to her lips, remembering the taste of him. She could still feel his hands on her thighs. She liked it too much. She couldn't be doing this again. She was always falling headfirst into a relationship, never questioning, never second-guessing. It had left her with a string of disappointments, and finally caught up with her with Henry.

"Wide-eyed optimism and wishing for the best," she said to herself. "That's for naïve little fools. He has a girlfriend, for Pete's sake. No matter how estranged, you need to stay away, Jesse. You're not ready for this again. You'll just make the same mistakes."

Finally, the valet drove up with her car. She tipped him five dollars and sped off. She wasn't sure how she was going to handle Cole. It wasn't as if she could erase him from her life now. She had made a deal with him, and would see him several times again before she could get him out of her life. More than what had just happened, it angered her that deep down inside, she knew she was still looking forward to seeing him again.

Cole hung the phone up, shaking his head. Another call ended in painful politeness. At least it wasn't the alternative, a fight. Why was he holding on? Why was she? It seemed like both of them wanted so badly to ask that question, to start the conversation, to get this over with.

Cole looked down at the phone and saw the reason why. He needed to sit face-to-face with Tracy and end this. He couldn't do it over the phone or in a letter. The coldness was too much for him. He had to fly to New York and handle the situation. But when? With the product and the murder, there was no time for that right now. He couldn't leave Chris to travel to the other side of the country. With Jesse . . . well, with Jesse, he just didn't want to be away from her.

Even if she detested him, thinking him a cheating bastard, he wanted to see her again. Even if there was no chance of touching her, kissing her again, he wanted to see her. Maybe it was a blessing that he had no chance with her right now. He had to focus on alert.com and finding those stolen documents before everything blew up in his face.

"Security is sending someone down for you right away."

Jesse nodded a thank-you to the woman manning the reception desk at the Netstyles building. She gripped her tape recorder in one hand and her car keys in the other. Her stomach was in knots.

All Jesse had been able to do over the weekend was think of her moments with Cole in his study. On his desk. It was amazing how she wanted to be angry and feel ashamed about it, but she was mostly aroused every time she relived the moment in her mind. She embarrassed herself. Even as experienced as she was sexually, she had never lost it like that, been so ready to do anything.

Now, here she was waiting for her Monday morning interview with Cole with so many butterflies in her stomach she thought it would burst. She had contemplated canceling it, but was too stubborn and proud to show she was so affected. So here she was, determined to keep control, but not confident she could.

"Jesse."

She turned to see Paul Brown approach her from behind the security gate. He was smiling, but looked tired and overworked.

"Hey, Paul." She accepted his hand and shook it. "On your way out?"

"No," he said, holding the door for her. "I'm here to get you. I was at our receptionist's desk upstairs when the front desk attendant rung up. When she mentioned your name, I remembered you from the funeral. I told the guard I would come for you."

"That was kind of you." Jesse followed him to the elevator, trying to calm her stomach. "I know you're all busy upstairs."

"It's kind of a madhouse up there." He flashed a security badge to prompt the elevator to the right floor. "What brings you by? Cole?"

Jesse suddenly felt defensive. "Why would you ask that? Has someone said something? Why would . . ."

He held a hand up. "Calm down. The receptionist was on speaker phone. She said you were here to see Cole. You had an appointment."

"Oh yes, of course." Jesse ordered herself to calm down. "I'm here for Cole."

"I hate to be nosy," he said, stepping aside so she could exit the elevator. "But can you tell me why? I mean, you come to me out of the blue at Sabrina's funeral, asking me weird questions. Now you're here to see my boss, who, along with his boss, has been treating me like I have Ebola ever since the funeral. I'm curious."

Jesse noticed extreme apprehension on Paul's face. "I'm interviewing him for a story on blacks in high tech."

They stopped outside the office with Paul's name on it. Jesse saw him relax a little bit at her answer.

"It just seems like everyone is keeping everything from me," he said. "I don't know what's going on around here. Chris has been a maniac."

"Chris Spall?"

He nodded. "He acts like a scared puppy one second and a raving lunatic the next. You should watch your back with those two."

Jesse smirked, laughing at the irony of his words. "I'm going to keep control. Besides, I'm only dealing with Cole."

"Usually Chris is not anywhere without Cole." He turned halfway to his office, then back. There was a look of hesitation on his face.

"What is it, Paul?"

"You were pretty close to Sabrina, huh?"

"Not very close, no. I just don't believe she committed suicide."

He scratched his head, his eyes distant. "Have the police done anything?"

"They seem to accept the suicide explanation."

"I'm sorry." Paul placed a hand on her shoulder.

He was obviously not an affectionate person, and Jesse could sense that this small gesture was incredibly taxing on him.

Cole stood in the doorway to his office, watching them. He felt a small tinge of jealousy just seeing her with him. And when Paul's hand touched her shoulder, Cole was surprised at the reaction it caused.

As if she were his woman. This was crazy. All weekend, she had been all he could think of. While he should have been concentrating on work since he spent the weekend in the office, he was imagining what would have happened if they had not been interrupted Friday evening. It had stirred reactions from him that he had not had in a long time.

He had been half excited, half dreading her Monday visit. She hated him, and was justified. Still, he would get to see her. And here she was looking as attractive as ever in navy blue shorts and a white-and-blue nautical cotton jersey shirt. Youthful, vibrant, and innocently sexy.

Jesse turned toward Cole's office and was stopped in her tracks when she saw him. This was going to be hard, Jesse thought. As she regained her stride, Jesse reminded herself she was here for an interview only.

"Hello, Jesse." Cole noticed her discomfort. What could he do about it?

"Cole." She nodded, avoiding eye contact. As she passed by him, entering the office, his sporty cologne caused a tickle in the pit of her stomach. *An interview only!*

"Please have a . . ." Cole didn't waste time finishing as Jesse went for the chair across from the desk.

"I thought it would be better if we sat on the sofa." He closed his office door. "It's more conversational, you know."

Jesse looked with apprehension at the sofa in the corner of the office. "Why do you want to sit on the sofa? And why did you close the door?"

Cole shrugged. "I was just trying to . . ."

"This is a professional interview." Stay calm, stay calm. "Please open the door."

He did as he was told. "I wasn't trying to make a move on you, if that's what you were afraid of."

She laughed, waving her hand. "Please. Don't be silly."

"If it bothers you, we can sit at the . . . the desk."

An awkward silence followed his last word. Jesse rushed to the sofa, wanting to be as far from the desk as possible.

"The sofa is fine." She sat on the end. "Can we get started?"

Cole sat at the other end of the sofa. He hated how much he wanted to touch her.

"This is ridiculous, Jesse. It's obviously awkward. Can we talk about Friday night?"

Jesse felt her stomach tense. "The contacts you gave me were great. I . . ."

"You know I'm talking about what happened in my study."

Jesse mustered the courage to make eye contact. "Nothing happened."

"Something happened, Jesse."

"Cole, I've told you I don't want to talk about it. I meant it. If you have any respect for my dignity, you'll let it go. I'm here for the story. Now, let's get started."

Cole couldn't ignore the injury to his ego. Still, she had every right to hate him, and he had no right to push.

Jesse turned on the recorder. *Stay calm, stay calm and professional.*

"Let's talk about you first, Cole. What led you to Netstyles and the chief architect position?"

Cole Nicholson was born and raised in Kansas City, Missouri. Both of his parents were teachers, since retired. No brothers or sisters. Always good with math and a whiz at putting things together, he received a scholarship to the University of California at Berkeley, where he majored in Computer Science. He interned after his sophomore and junior years at Technosoft, and worked there for two years after graduation. Receiving his MBA at Stanford, he became involved in the Black Engineers of Silicon Valley Association, where networking landed him a coveted position at Jennet-Dackard before he came to Netstyles when it was a virtually unknown company. It was here that he started Silicon City.

"Can you give me some examples of discrimination you have faced since this issue of blacks in high tech came out?"

Cole shook his head. "Jesse, I told you I don't complain about this stuff."

Jesse sighed in irritation. "Cole, this is important information. I'm trying to . . ."

"Next question." He tried not to smile at her angry stare. "Next question."

"Fine. Let's talk about women. Why isn't there equal representation of women managers in the workforce and women managers in technology?"

Cole felt like a lech. Here she was trying to be professional and all he could think of was getting his hands on her, his lips on hers.

"Cole?" Jesse felt the heat from his eyes. The way he was looking at her. "Women?"

He snapped back to order. "Simple. Technology is still a new industry. The people who are the most powerful are so because they know technology. Unlike other industries, it doesn't matter how much experience you have."

"What are you saying? Men know technology and women don't?"

He nodded. "Men have more technical backgrounds. You see, twenty years ago, men started in technical positions, whereas most women started in marketing, public relations, and human resources. You have your most recent generation of women and men who are equally into engineering, tech, computer science, math, and all that. They just aren't at a senior management level yet. It'll take some time to pick up."

"What do you suggest be done about it until then? Has anything been done?"

"We have to be patient. You can't force knowledge on people. You can only get companies to support the tools that will provide that knowledge."

"That would be how?" Jesse was having a hard time. He had to stop looking at her like that. She could feel her pulse racing.

Cole's eyes caught the healthy tightness of the skin above her neckline. His palms felt sweaty.

"Various ways," he answered slowly. He remembered how soft her thighs felt. So clearly, he remembered. "Such as Silicon City. Some companies in the area sponsor math and science tutors for high school girls. Their employees get extra vacation time or other benefits for volunteering as tutors. That sort of thing has really picked up since . . ."

"Stop it, Cole." Jesse turned off the recorder. She couldn't take it anymore.

Cole didn't have to ask her what she was talking about. He knew.

"Jesse, I . . ."

"This is crazy," she said, feeling her chest heave slightly as her breathing picked up. "I have to leave."

He reached for her, grabbing her before she could get up. He slid closer to her. "Jesse, don't go. I can behave. I know I can."

"Let me go." The electricity from his touch paralyzed her. She couldn't move.

He couldn't. Cole couldn't let her go. "I can't stand you hating me."

"I don't hate you," she said. "But this is wrong. It's unprofessional, too."

His hand slid up her arm, pulling her to him on the sofa. "I don't care, Jesse. I want you. Friday night may have been my fault, but I know you wanted me."

Jesse kept him at bay by pressing against his chest with her other hand. "It doesn't matter. What I want . . . what I wanted before was all wrong. It's too scary."

"Scary?" He slid close to her, his face only inches from hers. "Don't be scared of me, Jesse. I would never hurt you. All the things I could make you feel . . . fear would never ever be one of them."

When his lips came down on hers, Jesse's hands fell to her lap, her whole body went limp, and her eyes slowly closed. His lips were smooth and greedy as they took hers. Any attempt at tenderness was obliterated by desire that was too strong.

Her body drifted into a cloud as his lips turned her insides to Jell-O. His mouth, his lips were like a drug that she needed more and more every time she got a taste. The fire came so quickly to her belly, reason leaving her mind even faster.

Could she just give in? How her body wanted to. But no, she couldn't be so weak, so stupid. It was too soon, and his lips were too overwhelming.

She jerked away and jumped off the sofa, running out of the office. She heard him call after her, but didn't stop. Couldn't. It was all too much for her.

Just as before, Jesse felt herself on the verge of forgetting reason and propriety. With Cole, she seemed unable to think or do what was smart: jump heart first, or in this case, body first. But how could she without knowing she wasn't making the same mistakes as before? It was too much of a risk for her.

Too much.

Chapter Six

Jesse hadn't been able to find her tape recorder in three days. She was trying so hard to pay attention to Lita Quinn as she spoke about what it was like to be a woman in a male-dominated field. Jesse was really so grateful for the interview, courtesy of Cole's dinner party, but she wasn't into it. She hated herself for being so unprofessional, but for the past few days, the only thing she could think about was Cole. His lips on hers, his hands all over her. Him telling her that he wanted her and that he knew she wanted him.

She did want him. She wanted him more and more each day. And with the desire came the fear. Fear of past mistakes. Fear of future mistakes. She wasn't sure how honest he was being with her about Netstyles's connection to Sabrina.

And here she was, trying to listen and take notes. This was her job. She had to do this.

"So," Lita Quinn continued, leaning back in the chair of her casually furnished office. "To get back to the point . . . sorry, I tend to ramble on this topic. To get back to your question, yes, I do feel like I am paraded around by the company at times. Whenever something public comes up, they make sure their top ranking black female executive is highly visible. It offends me a little bit, but I use it to my advantage in two ways."

"What would those be?" Jesse asked, yelling at herself inside to pay attention. She felt so unprofessional. This really did matter to her. If it weren't for Cole! Never had a man been able to distract her from the rest of her life.

"For one, I can make demands on them now. This company gets good press and keeps the activist groups off their backs by having me. So, in order to keep me, it's had to be active in the community. Digital Oz does a lot more for the underprivileged than companies ten times its size."

"Do you feel they resent you for what you're . . . asking them to do?"

She shook her head. "Not at all. They got a little grubby at first. Nobody likes change. Nobody likes being told they were doing it wrong all those years. But, when it comes down to it, they know it's right. They see the benefits in their reputation, which leads to the almighty bottom line."

"Very smart. What is the other way?"

"The other you can see when you walk through the hallways at Digital Oz. When they throw me in front of the camera, send me to every publicity event, young men and women of color see that. They like that. With hundreds of tech companies hiring in this area, thousands in this country, seeing me can be the deciding factor in where they apply. I don't have anything to do with human resources, but I get about twenty-five percent of the resumes that come to this company. They're all from minorities and women who want to work here because they see me and feel they have a chance."

"I know it would certainly sway me," Jesse said, just as Lita's watch beeped.

She looked at her watch. "That's my time keeper. I've got a meeting with the head honchos in fifteen minutes. I have to prepare my notes, make sure my PowerPoint presentation is in order. You know the deal. Can't make a mistake. I'll walk you outside."

"Thanks a lot." Jesse stood up. "I hope we can talk again."

"Of course we will." Lita led her out of the office. "With you and Cole being a couple, I'm sure we'll run into each other at parties or social events. You know there are few enough of us that we keep a pretty close-knit group. Although I haven't seen Cole . . ."

"Cole and I aren't together." Jesse's eyes widened. The thought that they were being seen as a couple was all she needed. "We're just acquaintances."

The door to outside was only a few feet from Lita's department. The midday sun shone brightly on Lita's confused expression.

"Really? That's weird. I'm in public relations, you know. I'm a people person. I got from you two—you know, at the party last weekend—that you were . . . I don't know, close. Besides, Cole has never been a ladies' man. He usually won't bring a woman to a public event unless he's involved with her."

"He didn't bring me." Jesse realized that she felt some comfort in knowing that Cole wasn't a player. Why? It didn't matter to her. It shouldn't. "We met there. We're sort of working together on something. Besides, Tracy is his girlfriend."

"Tracy? Oh, yeah. I forgot about her. Haven't seen her in the longest. I just figured it hadn't worked out with her. They were too much alike, you know. Work is everything. Usually, someone needs to put love first to keep the other in line, if you know what I mean. To make it work out."

Jesse hated that the more she heard that Tracy wasn't a real part of Cole's life, the happier it made her. *You aren't ready for a relationship yet,* she told herself.

"I've got to go, hon." Lita hugged Jesse tightly. "Call me anytime. Cole or no Cole."

She was back inside before Jesse could even respond. *Cole or no Cole.* Was that what she had said? Jesse laughed at the irony as she turned and headed down the steps of the building. What she saw at the bottom, awaiting her, made her catch her breath and almost lose her footing.

"Hello, Jesse."

As with every time he saw her, her beauty took Cole. Today, in a simple white polo shirt and khaki slacks, with gym shoes nonetheless, she looked like a teenager.

Jesse tried to compose herself. "Cole. What are you . . ."

"I'm not following you," he said quickly. "I knew you'd be here. Lita called me yesterday to tell me you were coming to see her today. You left your tape recorder in my office. I came to give it to you."

She reached for it, careful not to let her fingers touch his. After putting it in her bag, Jesse said, "Why did you come down here to give it to me? You could have had it sent to me at the paper."

"That's pretty cold," he said, hurt that she would suggest

it. "Besides, things ended so badly with us Monday, I didn't feel we should just decide to ignore each other."

Jesse felt stupid standing in place, so she walked down the stairs, keeping a good distance from him. She was happy to see him again, and didn't know what to think of that. What was the old saying? The heart wants what it wants.

"How are you?" he asked, wanting terribly to know.

"I'm fine, thanks." *You are* not *happy to see him. You are* not *happy to see him.* She bit her lower lip.

He nodded at her. "I need to talk to you."

"Cole, I really don't want to talk about last weekend again. Or Monday for that matter. I said everything I had to say."

"I know." He'd left her alone for a few days, to let things calm down between them. But they really hadn't for him. He only ached to see her again. "But I wanted to talk about more than . . . than that. Something else."

Was there anything else in this world besides this thing between them? she asked herself. There hadn't really been for her the last couple of weeks. "What is it?"

Cole stepped aside for two women passing by. He hadn't intended on getting closer to Jesse, but that's what the move did.

Jesse immediately felt her body react to him. It was the equivalent of a chemical alarm going off.

"Can we go somewhere and talk?" Cole backed away, noticing Jesse's reaction. "Just across the street, where there's less people. Someplace public."

Jesse looked around to stall, but Cole was a determined man.

"What is this about?" she asked in acquiescence.

"Our agreement," he said, as they began walking no-where in particular down the street.

"I haven't forgotten, Cole. I've been busy these past few days interviewing those people for my story."

"I hope that's been going well for you."

She nodded. "Yes, it has, thank you. As far as my side of the bargain, I was planning on calling you later today. I just thought with . . ."

"It was best we kept our distance for a while." He wondered if she appreciated that he understood. "Can we sit down?"

They both sat down on a bench that had just been vacated by an elderly couple. Jesse calmed herself down. She found a sense of safety with all the people walking around them. It was the middle of the day, bright and warm out. She wasn't in danger of losing her senses with Cole next to her this time, was she?

"My schedule is pretty full this week," she said, partially making eye contact with him. He seemed to be getting more and more attractive every time she saw him. "As I'm sure yours is. Monday morning is the first day we can do this. It wouldn't take more than the morning."

"You mean you want me to take off work for this? Why not Saturday?"

She looked him over. "You're taking off work now, aren't you? My paper is a Monday morning paper. Saturday and Sunday are full. If you don't want to do it, I'm fine with that, too. Kept my end. I'm sure you think the office will explode without you."

"You don't know that it won't," he said with a half smile.

"I'm guessing it won't, but what do I know?" She liked his smile. It was genuine. "Now, do you want to observe these cases or not? I can do it without you and give you a report."

"No. I want to see this for myself." He did, but the truth was he wanted an excuse to spend more time with her.

"Fine, then. I made a list of all the files that involved any sort of threat or anything that would be considered dangerous. I organized them by location and timing. We can meet at Hakone Gardens, which is the location where Sabrina was beginning to spy on this new case that might have potential. It's a possible worker's compensation fraud. Those can be pretty serious."

"Sounds fine to me. Hakone Gardens at what time?" Cole was touched by the spark of excitement in her eyes as she spoke. He still wasn't sure how close she had been to Sabrina, but she was certainly committed to following up on this.

A jogging couple passed by them, bringing the beach back to Jesse. Would he ever mention that they first saw each other there? Would she? She was too scared to admit it. It would be as if just by acknowledging it verbally, she would be admitting how much she had been affected by it. She wished for the simplicity of those days. Strangers passing by each other, completely content with smiles and nods.

"What I could read of Sabrina's notes tells me she expects her subject to show her something around ten in the morning every day. Let's meet at twenty minutes to. Just in case he's early. If he shows, let's watch for his reaction. We want him to see us watching him. If he seems like he's going to get violent, then . . ."

Cole couldn't stand this. Whatever his relationship with Jesse would become, they couldn't do this. Sit here and pretend like it was nothing. "Jesse. I know I said I didn't want to talk about what happened, but I have to say something."

"Cole."

"No, listen. I can understand that none of it should have happened. I can accept that it never will again." That wasn't so much true, but necessary to say. "But I can't have you thinking I'm a cheating dog."

"I don't." She really didn't.

"Then can I explain?"

"Fine." Jesse was afraid to listen. Would he say something that would make her want to go against her resolve? Probably. She was such a softy when it came to this stuff. She begged herself to be strong.

"Tracy Neal is my girlfriend. We've been dating for about nine months. Only, three months ago, she got a consulting gig in New York. We've both always agreed that at this point in our lives, our careers still came first, so she went out there. It wasn't as if we were like sick teenagers in love before that. We enjoyed each other's company, had a good time. To make it short, since she left, we've visited each other a few times, but work got in our way. Recently, we've barely even talked over the phone. We've grown apart."

"But you're still together?"

Cole nodded. "Yeah, we are. But I'm going to make a trip to New York to break it off with her."

"That seems like the fair thing. For the two of you, I mean."

Jesse couldn't let him know that she was happy to hear from him what others had already been suggesting. "I am glad you explained it, even though I didn't think you were a cheating dog before then. You didn't intend for . . . what happened any more than I did. I just have to tell you that it doesn't make a difference to me."

Cole felt his heart sink into his guts. It was a long shot, but he was hoping an explanation would give him something, some headway with her even though those papers waiting for him on his desk told him that was the last thing he needed right now.

Jesse felt she owed him an explanation. "Since you're being honest with me, I guess I should do the same. When I seemed angry with you, it was just a cover-up. I was really angry with myself. No matter what your deal is, I'm not ready for a relationship or anything that would lead to one. I was just . . ."

"What, Jesse?" He sensed her hesitation and pain.

Jesse took a deep breath. Might as well let it all out. "I've only been in San Jose for six months. Before that I was in Chicago. I left Chicago because . . . my ex-boyfriend, Henry, decided that I didn't have a right to make him an ex. So, he spent about four months stalking me, threatening me, following me everywhere, breaking into my apartment, showing up at my job. He made my life a living hell. And the more I tried to stop him, the angrier he got."

"Sounds like he snapped." Cole felt a sense of protection for Jesse that only made sense with someone he knew and cared for deeply. Just hearing her say these things made him angry. "He didn't hurt you, did he?"

"Not physically." The compassionate tone of his voice, the sincere look in his hazel eyes, made Jesse want to tell him more. "Emotionally and mentally, he'd been at me since we started together. I was stupid and hopeful. I was certain that he was a wounded bird and my love would make him a different man. Next thing I know, a year had gone by and my entire life was a mess. His jealousy, need for control, and dominance had gotten to me."

"So you got out. That was what you had to do."

She nodded. "I did. But that's when the real terror started. He was relentless, and it all came to a head one night when he thought a coworker dropping off some papers was a date. I was lucky. He didn't hurt me. He was so enraged that he ended up hurting himself more than anyone else. He's in jail now for attempting to murder my friend, destroying my entire apartment by fire, and violating my restraining order for the twentieth time. So, I left Chicago because I just needed to get away. I have to admit that I'm still reeling from it all, and I'm just not ready to be with another man yet. I have some serious questions about myself that I have to answer."

"About yourself? You can't think you're to blame because this Henry guy went from jerk to psycho. If it hadn't been you, it would've been the next girl. That was all him, Jesse."

Jesse's eyes connected with his. She had been told this before, but somehow it meant more coming from him. She smiled and he smiled.

"Thanks," she said. "I know that, but it's nice to hear people say it. Sometimes I feel like everyone is saying, 'Stupid Jesse. Look at what she got herself into this time. Look at what she caused.' I just need time to think, get back to myself, and start a new life here."

Cole respected her resolve, her refusal to give in and be a scarred victim. "You'll have no problem with that. You're a survivor; I can see that about you. I'm not the best judge of character, but you seem like you'll be all right in whatever situation."

Jesse's eyes closed for a moment, her lips forming a

smile. She ignored the voice that told her she was slipping under his spell again. "I think so. What else are you going to do but survive? That's how I see it. I've made some great friends. I like my job. I'm getting involved in a lot of other things."

"If I can help you with anything," Cole said, wishing to God he could touch her, just to hold her. "You just let me know. As a matter of fact, I have a great real estate agent that can help you find that house you're looking for."

Jesse's calm was shattered. "What?"

It took Cole only a second to realize what he had done. He wanted to kill himself. "I . . . I mean you're new here, so you would be looking for one, right?"

"That's not what you meant." She felt a familiar shiver down her spine. A man invading her privacy, knowing things he shouldn't. "How do you know I'm looking for a house?"

"Wait a second, Jesse." Cole held up a cautioning hand as Jesse stood up. "It's not what you think. I didn't know who you were. I thought you might have something to do with the documents that were stolen from me."

"So you had me investigated?" Jesse's blood was boiling. She had been so stupid to think . . .

Cole had to make her understand. "All I knew was that you were somehow connected to the woman who had stolen documents about the most important thing in the world to me. I had to know who you were."

"How dare you!" Her hands clenched into fists. "How dare you invade my privacy like that?"

Cole stood up. "Jesse, I didn't know what I know now. I would never have . . ."

"That's a lie and you know it. You could never swear

on a Bible that you wouldn't do it all again. You would have done whatever you had to for your product. You're no different than Henry. Nothing matters but what you want."

Her words stung him. "No, I'm not. I'm not him."

"You invade my privacy and make me feel less safe than I was before. The only difference is, you do it legally. You're a creep, Cole Nicholson!"

"Jesse." Cole started after her, but she was fast and the street seemed to suddenly fill with people who walked between them.

He couldn't chase her. It would only make her think he was more like Henry. He had to fix this some other way. Had to. Because it became clear to Cole, as Jesse disappeared into the crowd, that he wanted her in his life. Needed her there. He was willing to wait until she was ready. The truth was, she'd been a part of his life since the first day he'd seen her jogging on the beach. But now, it was different. The reality of it all added an urgency to his feelings for her. She was the only thing that made him think of anything but alert.com. He needed that. He needed Jesse Grant.

The next several days were hard on both Jesse and Cole. Each of them tried desperately to keep busy to ignore the fact that everything in their worlds meant nothing. Both tried to think about anything other than seeing each other on Monday.

For Jesse, her story occupied her time if not her mind. Her interviews with Bill Castle and Brendan Astin led her to two stories for her series. First, minorities who have left the lily-white environment of the corporate world to start their own businesses. Second, how that first wave of publicity a few years ago created a Niagara Falls of online professional networking and job sites focused on minorities in the tech world.

An interview with a diversity recruiter for a Silicon Valley executive search firm shone a positive light for the storyline. The recruiter provided an outline of the increasing number of minority job fairs and the rapidly growing attendance of major companies at them, as well as the incredible growth in businesses like hers, which companies hired to find them minority managers.

Still, she couldn't escape Cole. Just as she would become immersed in an interview, his name would come up. Not to her surprise, Cole was well known and respected in the community. For the older crowd, he was seen as a symbol of the rewards of breaking down the barriers they had faced. For the younger crowd, he was seen as a role model, a standard by which to set and measure their own goals.

Jesse's heart only softened more as she found out that Cole had played a major role in the evolution of black protest against discrimination. In addition to participating in the traditional attempts of gathering outside buildings and writing CEOs and congressmen, Cole helped spread the word that the twenty-first century way to make change was to buy stock in companies and get black leaders on the boards of directors. Then minorities could speak with their financial and political power.

A man after her own heart, helping his people advance and move on. It was painful, feeling this affection and disdain for him at the same time. Now that she was hearing such good things, the disdain was getting weaker. What would protect her now?

Cole was having it worse. Up to his elbows in work, he

found that alert.com's early release was taking him from twelve-hour workdays to twenty-hour workdays.

Chris was making it harder on him by being unusually absentminded when he was present. Paul was making it harder on him by shifting from quiet paranoia to aggressive interrogations about alert.com. Dean was making it harder on him by bugging him about working too much and getting his feelings about Jesse out in the open. Tracy was making it harder on him by not returning his phone calls, his repeated attempts to meet with her face-to-face to end their relationship.

But Cole was making it harder on himself than anyone else. He kept going back and forth on what he wanted to do about Jesse. On one hand, he wanted to court and woo her. Sweep her off her feet and give her no choice but to fall madly in love with him and forget all about Henry and any other guy from her past.

On the other hand, he needed to stay away from her. Personally, that is. She needed time and space without him trying to make love to her, which seemed to be all he could think of when he was with her. He needed to stay away from her for himself as well. At least until everything with Tracy was cleared up, this craziness about Sabrina Joseph was put to rest, and alert.com was safely rolled out.

He wanted, needed to do something to lighten this load. Of the three, dealing with Tracy was the only thing really under his control.

So Sunday, after making his tenth call, and leaving yet another message, Cole wrote a letter. It wasn't the way he wanted to end this, but he couldn't wait any longer. Not with his feelings for Jesse becoming what they were. He had to do what was right. Something he should have done even before Jesse came into his life.

He wrote it like a conversation, trying to keep it from sounding cold and unemotional. The more he wrote, the clearer it became. He and Tracy had superficial things in common. And in the beginning of a relationship that was fine. Now, he realized that the parts of himself that connected with Tracy were the parts he wasn't so particularly proud of. Work was number one, achieve success at all costs.

He ended the letter with regretful apologies for not being able to end this better, to do this in person, but encouraged her to still call him if she needed to complete this over the phone. If it was what she needed. It wasn't what Cole needed. This was over, and his heart had made its obvious choice.

But he still had to keep his heart at bay. There was too much coming at him, too much coming at her right now. It just wasn't wise.

But when has the heart ever been wise?

Chapter Seven

Jesse's stomach tightened as she heard footsteps on the concrete behind her. She swung around. It wasn't Cole. Was he going to show? She looked down at her watch. 9:55 A.M. She was there. Would he be? She wished he wouldn't. Didn't she?

Hakone Gardens was a local treasure for Silicon Valley citizens. The sixteen-acre Japanese garden was built in 1918, and still held its original buildings, all replicas of early twentieth-century Japanese homes. The real attraction of the park were the beautiful gardens, with various types of Japanese styled manicures. The ponds running through the park and under its quaint bridges held turtles, koi fish, and other types of water animals.

It was a beautiful park, and busy every day. Classes and workshops on subjects such as haiku poetry, watercolor painting, a Japanese style painting called semi-e, and tai-chi were being held all hours of the day. In addition to that, the bridges and walkways provided a tranquil path for walkers and joggers.

The vibrating of her cell phone in her back jeans pocket alarmed Jesse. Everything was putting her on edge today.

"Hello?"

"Did he show?" Joan's voice came clear as day over the phone.

"Joan, I'm hanging up right now."

"No, wait!" There was desperation in her voice. "I'm calling for a legit reason."

"You've got five seconds." Jesse's eyes searched desperately around. Where was he?

"Luke wanted me to tell you about next Monday's edition. He wants to move your Latino celebration parade story to the front page."

"Front page?" Finally, some good news for a change.

"Don't get excited, Jesse. Bottom right. Far bottom right. He wants you to cut it to fifty words and make it a feature short."

"I'm going to strangle him! What's the point of having a diversity article if every story I do is treated like a filler feature story?"

"And all features have to be in by Wednesday or he says you don't run the story at all. He'll place an ad there instead."

"I'll come in tomorrow. I'm not giving in so easily. I'll bet you lunch tomorrow that by Wednesday the story is at least one hundred words."

"You're on. So, did he show?"

"I shouldn't have told you." Jesse regretted telling Joan everything about Cole. She had needed to get it out of her system and Joan was always a listening ear. The experience had been somewhat cathartic for Jesse. At least for a while. Until Joan ripped into her self-pity party and told her to either go after Cole or cut him out of her life completely.

"Yes, you should have told me," she answered back. "I can't believe you're falling in love and didn't want to tell me."

Jesse gasped. "I'm not falling in love. I never said that."

"You didn't have to. I'm not stupid."

"No, you're just crazy." Jesse sighed. "I've admitted to having feelings for him, mostly physical, but it's not love."

"Well, it's more than physical, so what is it then?"

"It's that same thing I always get when I meet a new guy. A sudden case of idiot's disease. I open the gates to my emotions without a thought or careful hesitation and get them shoved right back in my face."

"This time it's you shoving them back in your own face."

"I'd rather get over my own uncertainty than another man disaster. You know about Tracy, anyway." Jesse looked around some more. She couldn't believe he wasn't going to show. She felt her anger rising.

"She's a non-issue and you know it. You're acting like a baby. Playing scared to death."

"Maybe that's a good thing for a change. I have to develop a different method for falling in love. I jumped right into Henry, remember?"

"You're going to bring him up with every man, aren't you? That guy was a complete psycho. Is the comparison with Cole really valid?"

"Yes." Jesse paused and sighed. She knew right away that wasn't true. "Not really, but the whole thing with Cole having my background reminds me of the controlling, the deceptiveness. Henry was all fire at first. Cole . . . Cole is fire, too. Even more than Henry. Still, there's a comfort with Cole that I don't remember with Henry. I genuinely like the guy. I don't think I ever actually liked Henry. Was just crazy about him."

"See, there you go. You're coming around, girl. Now admit it. All that ranting and raving about how you hope he doesn't show up was a façade."

"Not completely." Jesse wasn't so sure of that either way. She knew what she thought, but she also knew how she felt, and as the hand on her watch turned to ten, she was disappointed. "I'm just not ready to deal with a relationship right now. And with him investigating me, I'm getting the creeps. I can't."

"It's not as unusual as you would think. Not in this day and age. Especially not in this city. Information is so easy and commonplace. Besides, like you said, he thought you were connected to Sabrina stealing his stuff."

"Why are you making this so hard on me?"

"Somebody needs to whip you back into shape. I don't want you to miss . . ."

"Joan, I have to go." Jesse unzipped her backpack on the table in front of her. She reached in for the file and kept her eyes on the man stretching at the edge of the bridge.

"Is it Cole?" Joan's voice sounded like that of an excited child.

"No, the subject is here. Talk to you tomorrow." Jesse hung up before getting a response. She looked at the picture Sabrina had taken and placed in the file. It was Andrew Lukansky, all right. In the picture he had his right arm in a white cast, held up by a navy blue sling. Today, no such thing.

Jesse grabbed her binoculars and felt a sudden surge of energy. This was exciting to her, and she wondered how it had made Sabrina feel. She felt bad, spying on a stranger, but at the same time right, catching a liar and a fraud. It was for these few seconds that she forgot all about . . .

"Hello, Jesse." Cole finally spoke after standing behind Jesse for some time. He enjoyed watching her, especially as she seemed to zero in on her subject. There was an energy about her that seemed to vibrate when she was excited. He had debated showing up today, knowing she wouldn't be happy to see him. But there were other issues at play.

First, if her assumptions were right, she could be putting herself in danger, and Cole couldn't bear the thought of anything happening to her. He was growing more and more suspicious of Chris as his behavior became more erratic, and he wanted to be convinced that there were other people who wanted to end Sabrina Joseph's life. A valued relationship was at stake there. Oh, yeah, and the fact that he couldn't think of anything but Jesse and had to see her again.

Jesse dropped the binoculars the second she heard his voice. She was too nervous to be embarrassed about it. She swung around to face him. Her heart sighed; she felt a tingle run through her body. He was so attractive. She just wished he wasn't so attractive.

"So you showed," she said in a very forced nonchalant tone as she reached down to pick up her binoculars.

"We did have a deal." He felt himself cringe as she turned her back to him. Fine. He had taken worse abuse than a snub. "Just because you think I'm a jerk doesn't get you out of our agreement."

"I never thought it would." Jesse couldn't even look at

him as he sat down on the bench next to where she was standing. "It's after ten is all."

"I underestimated the morning traffic in this area." Cole paused, feeling the air forming a thick molasses between them. *Here we go again.* "Jesse, I . . ."

"He's over there, near the bridge." Jesse couldn't bear it if he got serious on her again. She was not strong enough to deal with him as well as the feelings stirring inside of her right now. "This is the picture Sabrina took of him somewhere else. Can't read her notes on the back."

She slid the picture toward him as if to touch him accidently would be death. He just glanced at it. "Looks like it's outside the Tech Museum of Innovation on Market Street in San Jose. I want to . . ."

"I didn't bring my camera with me," she continued. Was he going to keep trying at this? "I wish I had. It really would help. Stupid of me not to think of it."

Cole frowned at her. "You're just here to see what Sabrina saw. Not do what she did."

"I know that." Jesse threw him a quick stubborn glance. "But I could do it if I wanted to."

"I'm not daring you, Jesse. You don't have to be so obstinate."

"I'm not being obstinate." She turned to him, feeling her temperature rise. "You don't have to be so bossy."

"How am I being bossy?"

Jesse mocked his words with a whining, childish voice. " 'You're just here to see what Sabrina saw. Not do what she did.' Like that wasn't your way of telling me not to even think about being a real P.I."

"You're nuts." He waved his hand at her. "You can do whatever you want. But from the looks of him, he's pretty strong. So, if he catches you catching him . . . be ready to run."

Jesse pressed her lips together and turned away. "I want him to see me looking at him. He's not even looking around like he's nervous or anything. The notes say he lives in San Francisco, which is plenty far away from here. He doesn't think anyone here will notice him."

Cole was taking his frustrations out on the situation. "What is this guy doing, anyway? He's been stretching since I got here."

Jesse heard her tone sharpen in response to his. "Maybe he's careful. He's focusing on his shins. Maybe there's a problem. Be patient, for Pete's sake."

"I'm not complaining," Cole said, annoyed. "I'm just asking a question. Besides, if he's not looking around, he's no threat."

"He could have been." Jesse didn't like the irritated vibe he was giving off. "If he did think someone was on to him, he might have been looking around suspiciously. That would be a sign that maybe he was on to Sabrina."

"Does she have a picture of him without his cast?" He reached for the folder, but Jesse held it away.

"No," she answered, "but he could have seen her when she was about to take one."

"And killed her." He smacked his lips and crossed his arms on the table. "Then returned right back here where her notes would lead police. We're wasting our time sitting here."

"Should I go up and ask him if he killed her? Would that speed things up for you?"

He didn't care for the attitude. "I came here to find out what was going on with Sabrina that could lead to her murder. I thought that's what you had planned for today.

But that doesn't seem to be so. You want to sit here and stare at people. Going to use your journalist's intuition as to whether or not they're killers?"

"Bite me, Cole." She glanced down at him briefly.

Cole bit his lower lip to keep from laughing. "Very lady-like."

Jesse swung her entire body around to face him. "You don't have to sit here! You can leave if you feel like your time is being so wasted."

"I just want a plan of action, Jesse." Cole appreciated her attention, even if it was her anger. "We're sitting here doing nothing."

"I'm sitting here being annoyed by you!"

"What now, Jesse?" Cole turned away, looking toward the bridge.

"What do you mean?"

He pointed toward the bridge. "He's gone."

Jesse looked around, cursing out loud. "Where in the hell did he go?"

"Let's just wait," Cole said, noticing Jesse's expletives were gathering attention. "Maybe he'll come back so we can stare at him some more."

Jesse's lips pressed together as she turned to him. "Shut up! This is your fault. You were bugging me to death and now he's gone."

"This was going nowhere anyway." He stood up. "What's next?"

"I just want to see what she was seeing." Jesse stuffed the folder back into her backpack. "Get a feel for what she was facing and get some idea of what she was getting into. Since you're so busy complaining, what was your plan?"

"I didn't know I was expected to have one. This was your baby. Your idea to even our deal."

"In other words"—Jesse placed both hands on her hips and tilted them to the right side a bit—"you didn't have a plan either."

"That's not true. I always have a plan when I'm responsible for something. This was for you to . . ."

"Just shut up!" She eyed him dangerously. "I'm tired of the sound of your voice. I'm going to the next case, and I don't want you with me."

"No dice, girl." He followed her, excited by the fire she was emitting, making him feel heated up. "We have a deal."

"The deal wasn't that you get to bug me to death."

"The deal didn't give me specific parameters, Jesse. I don't remember the deal saying you could tell me to shut up ten times in less than five minutes either."

"Well, maybe it should have, Cole. You need to hear 'shut up' a little more often. It would be good for you. As far as your parameters, I can think of a few. First being you can't bug me with annoying questions and snide remarks. Second being you can't investigate me and invade my privacy."

There was a thick silence between them as her comments settled in. Cole hadn't expected her to let it go. Still, the way she'd brought it up washed him over with guilt again.

"Can we talk about that?" he asked quietly, taking her by the arm and pulling her aside, away from the crowd that was beginning to jostle them.

There was that power surge again. Jesse felt it run through her entire body right from where his hands touched her. She fought to find her words.

"No," she whispered as he moved closer to her. "I don't want to talk about it."

"Then why did you bring it up?" His attraction brought on a flame in the pit of his belly with her so close to him.

"Because I had a right to." She looked up at him, wanting to kiss his lips. Wishing she didn't want to. "I still don't want to talk about it."

"Fine." He let her go. How would he ever handle this woman?

Jesse turned to walk away but stopped, turning back to him. She looked up at him again, catching his eyes with hers. "When I told you I was from Chicago . . . remember, when you asked me, and I told you I had only been here for six months? Remember?"

"Yes." He was touched by the emotion in her eyes. She was suddenly so vulnerable.

"You already knew, didn't you?" She felt tears coming to her eyes as she realized what it was that really hurt her. Not that he had found out so much about her. But that he had pretended as if he didn't know. Pretending as if she were telling it to him for the first time. As if he were making a joke of her revealing parts of herself to him.

Cole lowered his head in shame. He had really hurt her. Why couldn't he have seen that before? "Jesse, you have to understand. I didn't . . . when you spoke to me . . ."

"In your office on two occasions. At your party at your house," she said, reminding him of all the times they had been together. "On that bench outside Lita Quinn's office. All of that."

"I had read those papers, yes. But just for information on Sabrina or my product. When you were talking to me, I was hearing everything, learning who you were for the first time."

"Yes or no? Did you know all of that when we were together all those times?"

Cole nodded. "Yes, Jesse. I knew all about Chicago. I knew about your parents in Seattle, your brother in Costa Rica. I knew you had a restraining order out. I knew you had sold your house. I knew you had great credit. I knew it all. None of that mattered to me. I just wanted to know how you knew Sabrina. When I realized that you had no traceable ties to her, I got rid of it all."

Jesse held back her tears. "My life is mine. My past is mine. It's for me to decide who knows about it, how much, and when. It's not for Henry to invade and possess and it's not for you to tear through to satisfy your curiosity."

"What now?" Cole knew it was Jesse's call. He could only hope.

Jesse pulled at her backpack. "Now, we follow these cases and see what we see. We behave civilly with each other and go our separate ways afterward. Wish each other luck, I guess. No reason for us to fight."

Cole felt a knife cut into his stomach. She meant it. She didn't want anything to do with him. "I can't do that, Jesse."

"Cole, I . . ."

"I can't spend the day with you thinking I took something away from you. Knowing that it's too hard for you to be near me." He swallowed hard. "Go ahead on your cases, and don't worry about me. I'll figure out how to deal with my issues with Chris on my own. You do . . . whatever you need to do."

"I'm no more one to renege on a deal than you, Cole." Jesse felt a tug at her heart. She had started this whole scenario feeling she was the one who had been wronged. Now, she felt like the ogre.

"I'm doing this, Jesse. Not you. This . . . what is happening between us is more than the nonsense that we try to convince ourselves it is. Only neither of us can deal with it at this point in our lives. You, with your past still in your present. Me with Tracy and this crazy product. Then there's Sabrina. She's very alive and standing between us."

"So, it makes sense," Jesse said, her voice breaking a bit. If it made sense, then why was her stomach tearing into pieces?

"No, it doesn't. But it's how it is. As for me, I've ended things with Tracy, and I'm going on with this product. When it's over, when it's out there, I'm going to find that person who won't let me put anything between us. I hope one day you will, too."

Jesse's lips separated only a bit. She was speechless. She was falling in love with this man. The reality swarmed over her as he was turning his back to her and walking away. She was left alone, with strangers milling about. Left alone to realize that she was in love. It wasn't just the feeling that hit her, but the realization that she had fallen in love with him months ago. Her fall had begun that first day on the beach when she had jogged past him. That first glance, that first smile.

But now . . . now she was falling in love with the man, no longer the image or dream of a man that she had figured him to be. But just as quickly, he was gone. He was going to look for someone else. And that person, whoever she would be, was going to get the man that Jesse wanted.

"Joan was right," she said to herself as she approached her car. "You're such a fool. You're an indecisive little wimp."

She opened up her passenger side door and tossed her

backpack onto the seat. Just as she was about to shut it, her eyes caught a bright glare from underneath the seat. Bending over, she reached and felt around.

Paper, thick paper. She grabbed it. There were quite a few sheets. As Jesse shut the door, she leaned against her car, her mind having a hard time centering with thoughts of Cole and the opportunity she had just missed. She read some words here and there, not being of a mind to connect one word to the other. Until . . .

Seeing Cole's name on paper helped Jesse focus. She realized she was holding papers from the Netstyles file that Sabrina had left behind. While the file had fallen to the side of the seat, these papers had fallen out and under the seat.

The letterhead was from Netstyles. Notes from Cole to Chris Spall and someone named Brian Michaels. Rollout dates for alert.com, updates on the status of the chip glitches that were holding the product up. At the top of each page, in bold black letters was printed HIGHLY CONFIDENTIAL — ONLY TO BE READ BY ADDRESSEE. At the bottom of each sheet was a shred date. These papers had been intended to be shredded.

Jesse knew these were the stolen documents that Cole was seeking. She still could not imagine Sabrina having the guts to steal confidential papers away in the middle of the night, posing as a cleaning lady. She wondered what she would do. As she looked at the stack of sheets, she thought of handing them over to Cole. But the more she read, the more she realized what was going on. To spend her time following Sabrina's other cases was a waste. The juice was with Netstyles.

There was an entire sheet devoted to Chris Spall. He wasn't the family man that Cole believed him to be. Not at all. And Cole, based on Sabrina's notes, was the next subject on her list to investigate.

"Why?" Jesse asked herself, flipping through the pages. Finally, she found her clue. Its simplicity insulted her intelligence. How could she not have thought of this? Every case had a client.

Jesse hurried into her car and headed for Netstyles.

Paul Brown's eyes opened wide as Jesse stormed into his office. The no-nonsense look on her face was unmistakable.

"Jesse . . . uh . . ." His body tensed.

"You have some explaining to do, Paul."

"No one called me." He placed a pen over his ear and smiled. "You must be a whiz at getting past security. I have to go through hell every time I forget my badge."

"You can get anywhere if you want to badly enough." She came around his desk and leaned against it, only inches from him. She looked down at him. "You said you knew Sabrina from working out with her at the gym, right? Just passing acquaintances?"

"Yes, that's true."

"Then you don't know anything about her investigation of Chris Spall?"

Paul shifted in his seat. "I don't know what you're talking about. I'm very busy. I don't have time for interruptions right now."

Jesse tossed the stolen documents on the desk in front of him. She was giving him the copies she'd made only five minutes ago. She wasn't about to give up the originals. Not until talking to the police, at least.

Paul looked at the papers, leaning over the desk. He

started gesturing nervously, flipping page after page. "How did you . . . How do you know . . ."

"You hired her to spy on Chris Spall, didn't you? That's how you knew her."

Paul took a deep breath, still looking at the papers. "Look. I appreciate your journalistic zeal, but you have no idea what you're getting into."

"This is not about journalism." Jesse leaned closer to him, her eyes showing her anger. "This is about Sabrina. Now, I came here to give you a chance to explain this to me. Or, you can explain it to the cops."

His head jolted up. "You can't possibly think I killed Sabrina!"

Jesse paused, assessing him quickly. "No, I don't. But I think someone connected to this case, which you initiated, did kill her. And you know who that is."

Paul pressed his lips together in frustration and pushed back from his desk. He stood up and walked to the window, his hand pulling at an invisible beard. His hands formed fists against the window.

"I did meet Sabrina at the club. We talked. She knew what I did and I knew what she did. We used to work out and stop for health stuff at the Nutrition Center, the store below the club. This was all before I started getting suspicious at work."

"Suspicious of whom?"

"Chris and Cole. Who else? No one else here even knows about alert.com." He sighed, turning back to her. "The two of them finally decided to let me in on alert.com because it was just too much work for the two of them. Granted, most of what I did was the administrative crap they didn't want to, but I got to put together some good business plans and viable partnerships. I was promised that

I would get a part of a set-aside profit sharing for alert.com. That my options would increase."

"You started to suspect those promises weren't going to come true?"

"I couldn't get anything out of Cole. It was almost as if he resented that I had to know about it. Then Chris, well . . . you ask Chris a question and he has a way of charming you to death, so you don't realize until hours later that you didn't actually get an answer out of him."

"It's a very secretive project," Jesse said. "Maybe some things weren't a need-to-know for you."

"Everything?" The look of frustration on his face was evident. "Then, I realized that memos were being sent without my knowledge that I had been cc'd on in the past. I got really suspicious, so I asked Sabrina for help."

Jesse saw a guilty look on his face, which told her this was more than a business arrangement. "You were her lover, weren't you? You were the new lover her travel agent was telling me about."

Paul nodded. "Well, I wouldn't call us lovers. We hadn't consummated anything yet, but we were getting close. I was pouring out my fears and frustrations. She was going through a lot, too. I should have never put her in such danger."

"So you agree this was dangerous?"

"I figured I needed something to use as leverage with Chris. Sabrina was finding out all types of things about him that . . ."

"He was spreading it a little thin among the ladies. I read her notes."

"In the process, Sabrina was getting suspicious that Chris was involved in something that could be illegal."

"Like what?" Jesse's first thought was of Cole. Did Cole know? He couldn't. Whatever he was, he wasn't a criminal.

"I don't know. She never got to tell me. She said she wanted to get proof to show me. I never even got to see these papers you have."

"They were in her file, but they had fallen off to the side. I didn't find them until today." Jesse didn't remember Paul's name on any of those papers.

Paul returned to the papers, looking them over. "She was getting these for me. I wanted to know what was going on with alert.com. How Chris and Cole were planning on squeezing me out. They murdered her over these papers."

Jesse wouldn't believe that. "There is no way Cole is a murderer."

He turned to her, his face serious. "You know Cole would do anything for alert.com. In Silicon Valley, men and women will do all kinds of unimaginables to be the next hardware program or software product billionaire. For everyone you see, there are a hundred who he or she beat to the punch with pretty much the same product. Cole knows that. He practically threatened my life for the secrecy of this product. I had to sign a contract with some harsh penalties if I opened my mouth to anyone. Cole isn't playing around with alert.com. He and Chris are inseparable, and if they knew that some documents were stolen, the first thing on their minds would be . . ."

"Somebody is trying to beat them to the punch with a product."

"Exactly. Needless to say, the second they heard the documents were stolen, it was on."

Jesse eyed him carefully. "But murder?"

"Fine," he said. "Well, I'm at least certain that Chris had her killed, and Chris doesn't do anything without Cole knowing about it. Anyone around here will tell you that Chris and Cole are co-CEOs of Netstyles, joined at the hip. Don't let that silly chief architect title fool you."

Jesse felt her stomach tighten at the thought. "I'm still not buying that he was a part of Sabrina's murder. I would, however, believe that Chris had something to do with it. But if you're so certain, why don't you go to the police?"

Paul laughed. "You go right ahead to the police, young lady. They might humor you, seeing as how you're very easy on the eyes. But don't you think for one second you'll get anywhere. Cole is a millionaire; Chris is a multimillionaire. Their legal team can bury you or any prosecutor making forty grand a year. I need more proof."

"So, what are you planning to do?"

He grabbed a set of keys off his desk. "I'm going to get more proof. As a matter of fact, I've got an appointment to do that right now."

"And what would that be?"

He smiled at her. "Don't you worry your little head about it. I'll let you know when I get what I'm after. You and I can go to the cops together."

"If you want me to go to the cops telling them Cole killed someone, you'll have to have proof that would erase all reasonable doubt."

"What about Chris?"

"I'll listen to what you have first." Jesse noticed that his attitude was much different than when their conversation started. He was friendlier, more at ease now. "Don't get carried away. You don't have any proof yet. Those papers don't say anything about Chris's intentions toward you or Sabrina."

"You'll be hearing from me soon." Paul gathered up

the papers she had given him and placed them in a sky blue folder.

Alone in the office, Jesse searched Paul's desk for an appointment book. She couldn't find one. The drawers were locked.

With a snap of her fingers, she turned to his laptop.

"Yes!" His on-line calendar was still up.

NOON: TANAKA: TRADE BUILDING COURTYARD.

Who was Tanaka? Jesse didn't recognize the name from any of the papers. Appearantly, Paul was meeting this person at a fairly familiar location in downtown San Jose, closer to the south edge of town.

Jesse tried to decipher all of what she now knew. She wanted desperately to find out who murdered Sabrina, but wasn't at all prepared to blame Cole for it. She was falling in love with him.

Against her better judgement, she headed for Cole's office. She hoped to get some answers from him. She was probably the last person he wanted to see right now, but there was more at stake here than their feelings for each other.

Her stomach tensed when Cole's door was in sight. It was wide open, and she intended to walk right in. But just as she reached it, the sound of his voice, angry and irritated, stopped her.

"Chris, would you stop freakin' out!" Cole sounded like he was losing patience. "I told you I will handle Paul."

Jesse felt a chill down her spine at his words.

"I didn't say I don't believe you, Chris." Cole sighed. "It's possible that Paul has the documents, but I'm not getting why he would be blackmailing you."

There was a silence as Cole rolled his eyes. "Those documents don't hold any secrets about your personal life, Chris. It doesn't make sense. Look, I'm not going to argue with you about this now. Paul just went by my office. I have to find out where he's going. It'll only take him a few minutes to get his car."

Cole stood up from the desk, phone still at his ear. "Don't worry, Chris. Paul is not going to ruin this for us. I will handle him."

Jesse jumped behind a tall ficus plant just as Cole stormed out of the office. She could see him, but he couldn't see her. His forehead was lined with frustration and anger. His stride was anxious and determined. After he had gone, Jesse stepped out from behind the thick plant.

The hallway was closing in on her. She felt literally sick to her stomach. What was going on? She couldn't possibly believe what she had just heard. Jesse put her hand on the wall, supporting herself. She tried to think, concentrate on what was going on. There was no way this meant what she thought it meant.

Could Paul be right?

"Paul!" She said out loud. Jesse didn't know what was at the end of the road, but she knew she had to take it. She had to find out what was going to happen at the Trade Building.

Jesse parked her car illegally at the side of the building. She was too impatient to find a parking spot in lunch-hour traffic. She made her way cautiously to the courtyard. She saw Cole first. For a man with his presence and looks, it wasn't easy to fade into a crowd, though he was obviously trying not to be noticed. It was a large artificial courtyard at the base of a skyscraper, loaded with people eating lunch at its tables, stools, and benches. Jesse concentrated on Cole. She felt her senses come to life just at the sight of him. Despite all the misgivings she had about him now, none of that meant anything compared to her feelings for him.

Jesse found a bench and tried to hide herself behind the large gentleman on the other end of it. He was immersed in his lunch, with his Walkman blaring into headphones. She kept her sunglasses on, and had taken the straw hat she usually wore on the beach out of the trunk. She followed Cole's eyes. She had to lean a bit to her left, but she finally saw Paul.

He was nervous, or appeared to be, at least. He was talking to a man of Asian descent, very short, in a beige top and shorts that made him look like one little beige ball. Jesse assumed this was Tanaka. Paul's hands were waving in the air as he was explaining something. Tanaka just nodded.

Paul reached into his briefcase and pulled out an accordian folder. Jesse quickly turned to Cole, who sat up considerably, extreme curiosity on his face. For a second, Jesse thought he was going to approach the men, but he seemed to restrain himself. Turning back to Paul, she watched as he handed the folder to Tanaka. Jesse knew what the folder was, recognizing the sky blue color from earlier in the office.

Both men shook hands and walked away at the same time. Jesse watched Cole, wondering what his next move was. As she suspected, instead of following Paul, who hastily fled around the corner, he followed Tanaka.

Jesse wasted no time in following suit. Taller than most people in the crowded area, Cole was easy to follow while she still kept a distance. Jesse kept her eyes on him all the way out of the courtyard and onto the sidewalk. When he stopped, she stopped. She watched him grab a piece of paper and a pen from the back of his pants pocket. He wrote something down. Jesse wasn't sure what it was until Tanaka drove by in a brand-new Volkswagen Bug, almost neon yellow. Cole was writing down its license plate number.

What was he planning on doing with it? Jesse wondered. As he stuffed the paper and pen back in his pocket, Cole looked at his watch, and headed out the other way. Jesse watched until he got in his car, also parked illegally, and sped off. Hiding herself behind a family trying to decipher a map the size of a coffee table, she watched as he drove right by her.

Jesse refused to get scared. There was some explanation for all of this. There had to be.

Cole was beginning to hate Silicon Valley traffic. It seemed as if everyone in the area waited until he showed up to get on the road. His stomach clenched. He was trying to get Dean on his cell phone, but no one was picking up.

This was all he needed. He had not wanted to believe that Paul was behind the theft of the documents, but his intuition, the second sense that had served him so well in business and technology, told him that those documents were exactly what Paul had handed to that man. He knew he should be glad, because then his doubts about Chris would be erased if Paul was behind all of this. But if he was, why? Paul was good at what he did for a living, but he wasn't a greedy, diabolical person. Murder was way over his head.

"Hey, Cole!" Dean answered the third time his cell was called. "You just don't give up, do you? Three times in a row. I figured it must be important, so I might as well pick up."

"I need your help ASAP." Cole swerved through traffic. "I need you to find out about a guy."

"Look, man. Hold up. The last person I checked on for you turned out to be the hottie that has you tied up in knots, the person before that turned up dead. What's up with you?"

"No time for talk, Dean." Cole had no patience at the moment. "Can you do it or not?"

"For the right money, yeah. As long as it's legal. I'm not trying . . ."

"I have a license plate number. Can you get me something with that without breaking the law?"

"Yeah."

"Got a pen?"

"Always."

"Cali plates seven-eight-seven-nine-Y-one."

"By when?"

"An hour ago."

"Four hours."

"Good enough."

Cole hung up. He knew he had to let the frustration run through him if he was ever going to get past it. This day had started off on the worst foot with the argument with Jesse. Why had he walked away from her? Was his pride going to make him end up alone for the rest of his life? He had regretted it the moment he had done it, but had not tried to take it back. No matter how much he believed in what he said, he was not at all prepared to walk away from Jesse Grant. He had wanted to be with her from the first day he had seen her, and that desire had multiplied by a thousand now.

But why now, when everything else in his life was a hurricane mixed with a tornado? Why did she have to come into his life and completely take over his thoughts? Why did Chris have to completely unravel? Why did Paul have those stolen documents?

Why was he falling in love with Jesse Grant?

Chapter Eight

"I think you're overreacting." Joan stretched out on Jesse's living room sofa, her feet hanging over the edge. "You're making him into a killer."

"Do you think I want to?" Jesse's insides were a mess.

She had spent the last week trying to create scenarios in which Chris could be responsible for Sabrina's murder, but not Cole. When it came down to it, the two were inseparable, and it was killing her.

Joan twisted around to face Jesse, who was leaning over the lounge chair. "Actually, yes I do. I do think you want to make him a killer."

"Fine, Joan. Impart your wisdom to me." Jesse fell into the chair, her arms flopping to her sides.

"It's not wisdom," Joan said. "It's common sense. You have been looking for reasons to doubt yourself and your judgment since you got here. Believing that you are falling in love with a murderer would fall right in there. You're a nut bag who can't find anything but the worst guy out there. That excuses what happened with Henry and, therefore, why you need to stay away from men in general."

Jesse rolled her eyes. She was out of chocolate ice cream. It was the perfect companion for her self-pity. Now, Joan had decided to stop by before a Sunday evening out with Ray and was dragging her back to reason.

"Haven't you heard anything that I told you? Anything about Sabrina, her notes, what Paul told me? Cole and Chris?" Jesse jumped up, pointing a finger at Joan. "You! You were the one who said I should make sure Cole isn't just trying to distract me from suspecting him."

"Don't get your panties in a bind, girl." Joan waved her hand nonchalantly. "That was before. This is different."

"Why?"

"Because of all the kissing and carrying on."

"Because I kiss someone, it erases all suspicion?" Jesse realized Joan wasn't interested in listening to her side. "Come on, I'm serious, Joan. What if I've gone from a psycho stalker to a killer? What does that say about me?"

"You're stupid. You don't know anything. You have some serious problems, and you need psychiatric help."

Jesse was silenced. Joan's tone of voice wasn't joking.

"Finally, that's been said. It's what you've been wanting to hear forever." Joan rubbed her hands together. "So what does it all mean? Well, you're just like every other woman out there when it comes to finding the right man. Get over it."

"But I can't get over him, Joan." Jesse felt her body reacting at just the thought of Cole. "I can't get him out of my mind."

"Good. Finally." Joan stood up, walked toward her, and placed both hands on her shoulders. "I've listened to everything you've said, and I am not convinced. Do you want to hear why?"

Jesse looked up at her. "Do I have a choice?"

"Because you don't believe it for a second. There is doubt in every tone of your voice. Every syllable. You're like two people fighting each other inside. One wants to believe Cole is a murderer, the other wants to believe he's the man of her dreams."

Jesse nodded. "You're right. You're right. But I don't believe Cole is a murderer. I don't know how much he knows about Chris and what's going on, but he's not a murderer."

A horn honked outside.

"Finally!" Jesse exclaimed. "Please God, let that be Ray."

Joan grabbed her purse, following her to the door. "Very funny, Jessica. Don't try and act like you don't ache for my attention and input. Now, I'm going to go out with my man for a night of dinner, a movie, and who knows what else. You're going to stay at home, eat ice cream, and watch Skinemax. Let's not let this happen again next weekend."

"I will do what I can." Jesse opened her front door. "And I don't have movie channels. Remember, I work for Luke. I can only afford basic cable."

"You too? Oh, our suffering." Joan opened the door.

The joking stopped immediately when they realized it was not Ray about to knock.

Cole felt on display as both women stared in amazed silence at him.

"Hello, Jesse." He blinked, a gesture of humility. She

was adorable, even unintentionally in gray cotton tank top and white jean shorts.

Jesse finally found her voice, trying to ignore the frantic beating of her heart. "Cole."

Joan edged her way into the doorway, stepping in front of Jesse. "Cole Nicholson in the flesh. Nice to put a face to a name."

Cole smiled as the young woman looked him up and down. Slowly. She wasn't a shy one. "Yes. And you are?"

"Joan Griffin." She held out her hand to him. "I've heard a lot about you."

Jesse poked her in the back with her index finger.

"I'm afraid to ask what," Cole said. He was happy to know that Jesse was talking about him, whether it was good or bad. At least she was talking about him, thinking about him.

As the car honked again, Joan looked out at the street. "It is Ray," she said. "That's him right there. I'll tell him to wait."

"No, Joan." Jesse touched her arm reassuringly. "Go ahead. I'll talk to you later."

Joan's eyes narrowed as she came only inches from Jesse. She looked straight into her eyes. "Are you sure?"

Jesse nodded with an appreciative smile. "I'm sure."

Joan nodded back, waving her cell phone in Jesse's face. "Call me if you need me."

"I will."

Jesse found it hard to make eye contact with Cole. She didn't want him to see how happy she was to see him.

"Can I talk to you, Jesse?" Cole asked, after Joan was a good distance from them.

"Yes, I . . . yes." She stepped aside, letting him in.

Cole walked with confidence into the apartment. He

was determind that this encounter not end in another argument. He made his way to the living room sofa and sat down. He was facing the television, which was showing the early evening news.

"I didn't think I would see you again, Cole." Jesse wondered what she looked like. She sure hadn't cared at all this weekend about her appearance. He, on the other hand, looked his usual gorgeous self in a blue oxford shirt that hung down low over black jeans.

"I know, Jesse." Cole's hands felt like they weighed fifty pounds each as he rested them on his thighs. Maybe he should have sat on the chair. She was too close to him, only inches away on the sofa. He found it hard to think with her this close. "That's why I came over here. I've been doing a lot of thinking since Monday morning. I don't know why I hounded you so much. I know you're only doing what you can to find Sabrina's killer. I should have been more supportive. I was frustrated because I wanted something to tell me right away that Chris didn't do this. I wasn't getting that, so I lashed out at you."

"I should have planned it out better," she said. His heartfelt apology touched her so deeply, she was certain she was giving herself away. "A lot was riding on those cases. At least at that time."

Cole wondered what she meant by that. Did she know something new? Something new since last they had talked? "Can you forgive me for that?"

"No need to." Jesse smiled, feeling the room disappear. If he weren't so cute. . . . "You don't have to apologize for saying what you feel."

"That's just it, Jesse. What I said then, that wasn't how I felt. It was just what my pride forced me to say out of frustration and guilt. What I did—investigating you—was wrong. It was just wrong, no matter what excuses I tried to make."

"I blew it out of proportion," Jesse said, trying to control her excitement at his words. "I let my experience with Henry make me assume the worst of everyone. I know you weren't using that information to control me or anything like that."

"I shouldn't have had it in the first place." Cole slid closer to her on the sofa. "Jesse, you're all I've thought about since Monday. Hell, since I can remember. I don't know what this is we have. It's kind of crazy, but in a weird way makes all the sense in the world."

Jesse had to bite her lower lip to keep from screaming in happiness. Was this happening? It was, and she had not known until this very moment that it was all she wanted in the world.

"What about Chris?" she asked, unable to erase that thought from her mind. "Do you still think he's innocent?"

Cole pressed his lips together. "I . . . I've come to know a lot about Chris in the past few weeks that makes me wonder if I really know him. But I have to be honest with you. My overall opinion of the man hasn't changed. He's not a murderer."

"Cole, he's connected somehow." Jesse had read Sabrina's notes—those she had found under the car seat with the stolen documents—several times this weekend. "You have to believe that."

"I don't." Cole turned away, his hand clenching into a fist. "Jesse, I don't want to discuss Chris right now."

Jesse was hurt by his physical rejection of her. "Why? Because you feel you owe him? You've paid him back tenfold by putting his company on the map."

"Jesse," he said, turning back to her. "Let it go."

Jesse socked the sofa with her fist. "I can't. You just don't want to deal with it because of alert.com. Sabrina was a person. People are more important than software products!"

"I know that, Jesse!" Cole felt his frustration grow.

"Show me, Cole. Show me that you know that!"

Before Jesse could react, Cole grabbed her by the arms and pulled her to him. His lips came down on hers with force, and the passion hit Jesse like a lightning bolt. The anger in his lips only served to excite her, and she lifted her hands to his face, kissing him back.

His desire was ravenous, and as his hands moved to her body, all Cole could think of was making love to her. As his lips ravished hers, his hands caressed her breasts gently. He could have never prepared himself for this feeling, as it took him over like a possession.

Jesse's insides were water, her entire body an inferno. She felt his tongue hot in her mouth and her belly was twisting and turning. She pulled at him and leaned back at the same time. She wanted to feel his body against hers.

Cole's body was aching at this point. It was some kind of painful pleasure he could not remember ever feeling before. As she lay back, he looked down at her. Her eyes were hazy and half closed. He studied her lips, her breasts . . . everything.

"Jesse, you are so beautiful. I want you so bad."

"Then take me, Cole." She grabbed at his shirt, pulling him down on her.

His lips dropped kisses on her mouth, her cheek, her chin, and slowly onto her neck. His hands gently slid her tank top above her breasts. His tongue teased the left breast, circling her nipple as his hand cupped the other breast. He wanted to savor every sweet taste of her.

Jesse felt like her body was going to explode. It had been so long since she had been with a man, but even then she had never wanted one so badly. Her body wriggled under his in anticipation and she bit her lower lip as his mouth tantalized her breast, his hands rubbing at her waist.

The tender pain of his teeth at her right nipple forced a loud moan from Jesse and her body turned at the charge. Unfortunately, her sofa wasn't very large and the both of them went flying to the floor.

They hit the floor with a thump, both grunting at the pain. Cole tried to lift his head up, but the coffee table was in the way, and he yelled out a curse as he hit it.

"Oh, Cole!" Jesse was so confused. She was still filled with desire but now pain and laughter hit her. "Are you okay?"

Cole gritted his teeth, one hand at the back of his head. "I think I'll be okay."

Jesse used the sofa to help lift her up. She pulled her shirt down. "I guess the sofa isn't the best place for this."

Cole stood up, still with only one thing on his mind. He reached for her. "Where is?"

At this point, for Jesse, anywhere would be fine. "My bedroom?"

She turned and headed for the hallway. Cole began to follow, but stopped suddenly, slapping himself on the forehead. "Dammit, Jesse. I don't have any . . ."

"You don't?" Jesse felt her heart sink.

His smile held humility. "I don't keep them handy. I usually don't get an . . ."

Jesse kissed him affectionately. "I don't do the one-night-stand thing either. I'm glad you don't. I've got to have something. Let me check the bathroom."

As Jesse darted for the bathroom, Cole headed for the bedroom, which he assumed was at the end of the hall. His mind a haze and blur of passion, desire, and emotion, he almost missed it as he walked by. Almost.

The Netstyles letterhead was unique. Chris had created the insignia with a gigantic *N* and the *etstyles* wrapping in a circle around it. The words were an eggplant purple and the design of sparks emanating from the letters were banana yellow.

Cole tried to concentrate as he reached for the papers on the living room table. They were spread out all over the table. With his whole being concentrated on making love to Jesse, it was hard for him to understand what this was. He blinked several times and took a deep breath.

"Concentrate," he told himself, amazed at the effect that woman had on his system.

The rest of the world zapped back to him as he realized what he was looking at. They were the documents he had been looking for. The stolen documents! These were the originals! What were they doing in Jesse's apartment?

"Cole, I . . . " Jesse held the tiny package in her hand, ready to wave it in the air. All she wanted was to be back in his arms, to make love to him, to be lost in oblivion with him.

Only Jesse knew from the look on Cole's face as he turned to her, that was out of the question. She looked at the papers in his hand and wanted to panic.

"Cole, I can explain that." She ran to him, to the table. "I just found . . ."

"What are you doing with these?" Cole couldn't believe it. "You know I've been looking for . . ."

"I just found them. I swear. I was going to tell you about them, but you were so angry at me."

"What does that have to do with anything? How did you find them? When?"

"Just Monday," she said, not sure what meaning to take from his words. "After we fought. I guess they fell out of the file that Sabrina had on Netstyles."

"Mysteriously missing from the file you gave me," he said, his voice laced with suspicion and disbelief.

Jesse was stung by the tone of his voice. "No, Cole. I just found them Monday. I'm telling you the truth."

Cole turned away from her, trying to calm himself down. He could not take this out on Jesse. His heart did not want to be mad at her for anything, whether it was her fault or not.

"Cole," Jesse reached out, touching his shoulder. She couldn't stand him being this angry at her. "I was going to return them to you. I was."

"I believe you," he said, gathering the papers up. "I'm sorry for yelling. I just wish you had brought them to me right away."

"I should have, I know. It's just that Paul needed time. And when I realized that he hired her . . ."

"Paul did hire her?" Cole's eyes lit up. Chris was right. "How do you know that?"

Jesse pointed to the sheets of paper with Sabrina's notes on them. "It's not easy to read, but it's all here. Paul hired her because he thought Chris was . . . Cole, there's a lot of stuff about Chris in there that you might not want to read. Paul told me that . . ."

"Paul is a liar." An image came to Cole's mind, images snapping together. "When did you talk to him last?"

"Monday afternoon." Jesse could tell Cole was working

something out upstairs. "We talked about these documents. He cared about Sabrina. He . . ."

"He wasn't upset that you had them?"

"He didn't know I had them until Monday."

Cole was confused. "So, he hired Sabrina to find out some dirt on Chris? Maybe that he was having an affair. But why would he want Sabrina to steal documents on alert.com?"

"He thinks Chris was trying to squeeze him out of the agreement you made with him about his share of the profits." Jesse swallowed hard. "He thinks you were, too."

Cole's brows rose. He studied Jesse's face. She was concerned. "Jesse. I wasn't at all interested in scamming Paul. I just didn't think he needed to know what was going on outside of his responsibilities. Paul's a smart guy and good at what he does, but I'm not certain of his character and how much I can count on him."

"But you are of Chris?"

"Enough to know I can tell him what's going on," Cole said. "But back to what I was asking. Apparently Sabrina stole these documents, but Paul is saying that he never saw them?"

"I believe him." Jesse saw the skepticism in Cole's face. "I do. I'm sorry. Why would he kill her if she was finding stuff out that would help his cause? Besides, they were close to being lovers."

"Jesse." Cole sighed, a part of him loving the trust she had even though it might be clouding her judgment. "Paul is up to something. I saw him meeting with a man Monday afternoon. He gave him papers, and . . ."

"I saw you." Jesse threw the truth out there before it was too late to bring up. "I saw you at the courtyard following Paul. I was following you."

Cole was stunned into silence for a moment.

"You're following *me* now?" he asked.

"Paul told me he was going there and I knew you were following him. He met with that guy, Tanaka. He gave him copies of these documents."

Cole's eyes flew open. He tried to control his anger. "Dammit, Jesse. I knew that's what he was giving him. Why did you give Paul a copy?"

"Paul is not the enemy here," Jesse said. "He doesn't want alert.com sabotaged either. He stands to profit only if you guys get it out faster than everyone else."

"That man he gave it to, Adeki Tanaka. He's a private investigator."

"You took down his license plate and had him investigated." Jesse eyed him sternly.

"This is serious business," Cole said. "Besides, Chris had him investigated after I told him what happened."

"You told Chris about Tanaka?" Jesse wondered now if Cole had placed Paul in danger.

"I'm sorry if you don't like that, Jesse, but Paul is giving confidential information to strangers and hiring them to sabotage us. I had to tell Chris."

"Paul hired Tanaka for the same reason he hired Sabrina. To find out how Chris is screwing him. You've both abandoned him, so he had to go elsewhere. Chris found out and he had Sabrina murdered because of what she knew about alert.com and his private life."

"No way, Jesse." Cole turned away, not wanting to hear this. He didn't care what those papers said about Chris's private life. As long as he wasn't a murderer. That would be too much for Cole. "There's another expla—"

Jesse turned to the television, which was what obviously

caught Cole's attention. She gasped at the picture on the local news program.

"The victim is Adeki Tanaka," the correspondent said somberly. "He was a private investigator, found murdered in his office on Adams Street, just south of downtown San Jose. He was shot once in the head from behind, late yesterday afternoon. Currently there are no witnesses, but police are asking that anyone . . ."

"Oh my god!" Jesse was shocked. "Chris killed him. You told Chris about Tanaka and he had him killed."

"That can't be." Cole gripped the papers in his hand tightly, wringing them together. "No. This doesn't make sense."

"It makes perfect sense," Jesse said. "You told Chris about Tanaka. Chris had him investigated, found, and murdered. He's trying to hide whatever these investigators are on to. And now that you've told him Paul hired them, I'm sure he's next."

"Quiet!" Cole rushed to the television as the correspondent spoke more.

"The area in which Tanaka works has one of the lowest crime rates in all of Silicon Valley, so police are looking beyond the random violence angle. They report that nothing was stolen. Several files that Tanaka, a former police officer with the San Francisco police department, was working on were confiscated. Investigators believe the answer to his death lies there."

Cole had to find Chris. "This could be awful. What if they have our documents? The police don't care about our competitive advantage. They'll let everyone and anyone see them."

"So now you think the police are trying to hurt you?" Jesse saw a hint of panic hit Cole. It wasn't a position he was used to being in, she could see that. She hated herself for her part in all of this.

"Jesse, you'd be surprised how many Internet tips are gotten through police, package delivery men, mailmen, and the like." He reached for his cell phone and pressed a speed dial button.

"They probably don't even have your file," Jesse said as she followed him to the door. "Chris certainly took them after he killed Tanaka. That's what he was there for."

Cole turned to her, anger clearly on his face. "I know what this looks like, but I don't believe Chris is a murderer. I just don't buy it."

"Buy it or not, I think it's plain. Are you going to let your desire for this product to make you rich hide the truth of what's really important?"

Cole pressed his lips together. He heard Chris's voice on the other end of the phone.

"Cole!" he was yelling. "Cole, are you calling me?"

He looked down at his phone. "Jesse, I have to go."

"I know you do," she said. "I'm sorry this is happening to you, but I think you're making a mistake by choosing to stick by Chris. This has gotten out of hand, and has reached a point that is more important than any Internet product. You have to choose."

"I haven't gotten where I've gotten in this world by making choices based on emotion, Jesse." Cole headed for the door.

"You think you can have it all. The truth, justice, the product, the company, the money."

"And the girl," Cole said, smiling at the spark in her eye as he said those words.

Jesse's frustration made way for excitement at his last

words before leaving. Even at a time as desperate as this, he could make her feel this way.

Jesse glanced around at her apartment, which seemed bigger and emptier than usual. She fell onto the sofa and ran her hands over the seat. She closed her eyes, reliving the scene of passion she and Cole had just shared there, then on the floor. She realized that if he hadn't seen those documents, they would be in the throes of passion right now.

She sighed, knowing just how satisfying that would have been. With a smile, she ran a hand over her hair, while using the other to fan herself. She felt his hands all over her again, his lips all over her body, his tongue in her mouth.

Then, she thought of why he left. Adeki Tanaka was dead, so was Sabrina, and Jesse didn't doubt for a moment that the same person was behind both murders. Neither did she have much doubt that it was Chris Spall. It was not that she wished this on Cole, knowing how he felt about Chris. There was also the fact that her stupidity, showing those papers to Paul instead of Cole, was to blame for Adeki Tanaka's murder.

She knew Cole was going to follow Paul to his meeting with Adeki no matter what Paul had to hand over to the man. But she also knew that Cole reporting to Chris that Paul did hand over what they were looking for could have pushed Chris over the edge.

Jesse wondered how this would end. Was Paul in danger? Was she? She didn't even want to think of that. If Chris was all Paul made him out to be, then he was in big trouble. Did that mean that Cole was in trouble, too?

"What have you done, Jesse?" she asked herself, no longer feeling the euphoria of Cole in her arms again. "What have you started?"

* * *

"What took you so long?" Chris Spall asked as he opened his front door to Cole. "Come on into my study."

"I was headed right over here from Jesse's house, but I had to stop to do a little summer reading." Cole's tone was harsh, but he kept his voice down. He knew Chris's wife, Sherri, was somewhere in the house, and she had a habit of showing up out of the blue.

"What do you mean?" Chris closed the door behind them as they entered the classic old English style office. "You talking about the newscast?"

"I'm talking about this." Cole tossed the papers onto Chris's desk. He waited for Chris to start reading. He knew the sheets with Sabrina's notes were on top.

On the phone in the car after leaving Jesse's, Cole had been told by Chris to get over to his house immediately. He didn't want to discuss anything over his phone, because, in his words, "I can't be sure the line is clear." Cole hated the level of suspicion that had risen in him, but Tanaka's murder gave him no choice. So Cole had pulled over and read Sabrina's notes on Chris. What he read made him sick to his stomach.

"I can't believe you have two mistresses, Chris." Cole didn't try to contain his disgust. "You have a child with one of them."

Chris shook his head. "Cole, I can explain all this."

"Unless it's all a lie, I don't think you can." Cole threw his hands in the air. "I can't believe all of what I read. Tell me if it's true, and don't you dare try to lie to me, either."

"I have a weakness, Cole." Chris sat down in the desk chair and laid his head in his hands. "Women are my weakness. You know what it's like when you have money. There's never any shortage of them around."

"You have a wife!" Cole caught himself and lowered his voice. "You have two children. How could you? Does Sherri know about this daughter of yours?"

"Of course not." Chris looked up. "She would drop me like a sack of potatoes. I love her, Cole, I . . ."

"I don't want to hear that crap! Chris, this isn't about me believing in you, because I'm a grown man and I can deal with disappointment. But all of this gives you motive."

"Motive?" Chris's exasperated expression made him look ten years older. "I did not kill anyone."

"I want to believe you, but I . . ."

"Then do. If not for me, then for our company, our product—"

Cole shook his head. "Chris, Netstyles isn't the most important thing in the world. Not anymore."

"Yes it is, Cole." Chris's eyes narrowed, his expression like a cornered cat's. "Don't tell me you've let this . . . Jesse make you lose sight of that."

"Yes, I have. And I'm grateful to her for that. What's right is what's most important. Finding out who killed Sabrina is what's most important."

"That's fine." Chris stood up, waving his hand around. "We'll do all that after alert.com is released."

"We'll do it now, Chris." Cole slammed his fist on Chris's desk. "Jesse could be in danger and I will not let anything happen to her. Not for you, not for myself, and not for any amount of money."

"You know, principles are good things. And they do have a place in business. But you should also know when it's time to set all principles aside for the bottom line. And alert.com is one of those times. I've always been concerned about your ability to do that. This is your chance to prove yourself to me."

"No, Chris." Cole stood up straight and looked his boss in the eyes. "I've proven my ability to run Netstyles and make it the company you have always dreamed it to be. I've done that ten times over. Now is your chance to prove yourself to me."

Chris's eyes were desperate. "Cole. It's you and me, remember? Three years ago, we made a commitment to each other."

"You made a lot of commitments you haven't kept." He nodded to the picture on his desk of Sherri and the children. "You tell me now, and tell me everything. Is there more to what Sabrina was investigating than just the smear to your good name?"

Chris lowered his head. "No."

"You had *no* plans to cheat Paul out of any of the agreements we made to him for his contribution to alert.com?"

"No."

"What about an explanation for Paul getting Sabrina to steal from Syndot's offices?"

"He's up to something, Cole. I'm telling you. But I don't know exactly what. We need to get rid of him." Chris reacted to Cole's surprise at his words. "I mean fire him. We need to fire him."

Cole contemplated whether or not he wanted to believe anything Chris said anymore. He wanted to believe Jesse. Not just because he was falling in love with her, but because she was a smart woman with a good instinct, and an even better heart.

"No, Chris," Cole said. "We don't need to upset Paul

until we figure out what he knows, what he's done, and what he suspects of us. We need to keep him close."

"What about the police?" Chris asked. "What if they start getting in our business?"

"I'm going to get Alice Simms on it right now. That's what public relations people are for. The papers Tanaka had only suggested you might want to kill him because he could expose all your personal indiscretions, not alert.com. What was on there didn't discuss anything about alert.com or its launch that could be seen as a violation of contract. Because there is none, right?"

Chris nodded. "Yeah, right. Of course not."

"I'm going to see what Dean can find out from his police contacts. Maybe our file wasn't in that pile the cops collected and this is all for nothing."

Cole eyed Chris carefully to gauge a response to his words. Chris nodded as if uninterested in discussing it further, and that worried Cole. For him not to respond to the suggestion that the file on Netstyles might still be out there made Cole wonder if Chris knew it wasn't. Maybe Chris had it.

"Good night, Chris."

Cole didn't wait for a response before leaving the office and leaving the house. He was dialing Dean on the phone while pulling out of Chris's enormous driveway. He didn't have time to feel sorry for himself, to be afraid of losing out on alert.com, or to feel hatred toward Chris for deceiving him so deeply about the man he was. He had to figure out what made Paul so suspicious of Chris, and what the police knew about Netstyles. Most important, he had to make sure the woman he loved was safe.

* * *

Jesse was surprised to see a woman open the door to Cole's house as soon as she arrived. She had robbed Jesse of the chance of banging on the door as she had intended.

She was an older woman in her late forties with hair that was strawberry red, except for a streak of white down the entire left side. She wore no makeup except blood-red lipstick, and dressed like she was on her way to the beach.

"You must be Jesse," she said with a soft, Southern voice. She was utterly charming with a sweet smile and batting lashes. She held her hand out to her. "I'm Alice Simms."

Jesse nodded to the woman as she shook her hand. She had no right to ask for more information. Cole was not her man. He could have any woman he wanted in his home. However, the expression on Jesse's face must have given her away.

"It's nothing like that, dear." Janice stepped aside to let Jesse in the house. "I work for Cole. With all that's been going on, we've been holding meetings at his house. There's too much press at the office."

Jesse suddenly recognized her name from the newspaper reports of the last few days. "You're the public relations director for Netstyles?"

She sighed, rolling her eyes. "Yes, I am, honey. A tired one at that. Oh, well, I suspect you know your way in. He's in his office. I'm off to the coliseum to fight the lions. You will root for us Christians, dear, won't you?"

"Of course." Jesse smiled at the woman's belle charms and said her good-bye as Alice headed for her car in the driveway.

Jesse tried to recapture some of the anger she felt as

she headed for Cole's office. It was Wednesday afternoon, three days since her last encounter with Cole. She had only heard from him once, when he'd left a message on her answering machine telling her he'd hired a bodyguard to follow her around until everything was figured out, whether she liked it or not. Jesse had noticed the man outside her house and the Silicon Valley Weekly's offices.

Besides that, nothing. Jesse had left several messages wanting to talk to him, but none were returned. What had transpired over the past few days alarmed her tremendously. The files on Netstyles had been found by the police. The *Mercury News* quoted a leak as stating that they were the only files hidden underneath a secret slot inside Tanaka's desk. All his other files were in the cabinet. Due to the unique location, Netstyles became the main target of the investigating group.

Not much was said about alert.com, since the police really had nothing to go on based on the documents, which were not too decipherable to anyone other than the people involved in the product. But much was said about Chris Spall and his private life. According to the paper and the nightly news, he was the main suspect of Tanaka's murder. No one had connected Sabrina Joseph to any of it yet.

"Jesse." Cole placed the bottle of Scotch back down on the bar when she entered the room. He never drank hard and never ever drank during the day. But recent events made liquor a tempting source of comfort. She had saved him, and he was happy to see her. "You're here."

"Surprised?" she asked with a sarcastic tone. Her heart ached at the sight of him. He looked like another person, ragged, worn down, and tired. "Of course not. Seeing as how I've been leaving message after message with you for days, how could it be a surprise?"

He smiled at her feistiness. He had missed that and every-thing else about her in the past few days. He had thought of her often. Too often, considering everything else. "I'm sorry about that, Jesse. You have to understand what's been going on. You've been reading the papers, listening to the news."

She nodded as she sat down in a chair next to the bar. "You thinking of drowning your sorrows?"

"No." Cole put the cap on the bottle of Scotch and pushed it away. He sat in the chair next to her. "But God, I'm happy to see you."

"I know you've been going through a lot, Cole, and I hate to take more out on you, but I'm very disappointed in what's been going on."

"You are?" He laughed out loud. "Join the club, honey."

"What Netstyles is trying to do is cover up for Chris."

Cole frowned at her. "Don't start with that, Jesse. Right now, I don't need another anti-Chris session."

"I know a lot the rest of the public doesn't know, Cole. The crime-beat reporter for our paper has a lot of contacts at SJPD and knows things the *Mercury News* doesn't print. Not yet at least. Chris is the number one suspect in Tana-ka's murder, and your lawyers are trying to cover up for him. What you guys are telling the press is that he's not even close."

"He's not, Jesse." Cole didn't want to get into this. Not after what he had just found out from Dean.

"This alibi you guys are making for him is flimsy at best."

"It's still the truth." Cole sighed. "Jesse, can you let this go? I haven't gotten any sleep in three days. I've been running a company, moving my product along, and deal-ing with angry investors and press sharks."

Jesse felt compassion for him, but she couldn't let it go. "Well, Sabrina Joseph and Adeki Tanaka are dead. But I guess that's not as important as your product."

"Dammit, Jesse!" Cole shot up from his seat and knocked over a glass on the bar. "I don't need this now. Not now."

Jesse's mouth flew open. She wouldn't have imagined Cole reacting like this. Something was terribly wrong. Worse than what even she knew. She stood up and walked over to him, placing a comforting hand on his shoulders. She felt his tense muscles loosen up under her fingers. He turned to her.

"I'm sorry Jesse." Cole gently brushed her cheek with his finger. She was so genuinely concerned for him, and it touched him deeply. He had lost his temper with her, and that was the last thing he wanted to do.

"What's going on, Cole?" she asked. "What is it that's really getting to you?"

"I just spoke to Dean a few minutes ago." His hands clenched into fists. "I wanted to trust Chris. You know, I love the guy. He looked me in the eye and told me there was nothing more to this than Paul's paranoia. He wasn't trying to steal from Paul and he wasn't behind anyone's murder."

"But you needed to prove that to yourself?" Jesse saw the pain in his eyes. He felt guilty for not believing Chris even though in her mind, Chris didn't deserve his trust. "You're a loyal man, and that's a good thing. Sometimes you have to make decisions that make it appear as if you aren't. But you still have to."

"I had Dean investigate Chris's . . . relationships. The younger mistress, Alicia Brody, has a daughter by Chris. You read it all in the papers. What you haven't read, and what Chris didn't tell me, is that he's been having a hard time providing for the child in a way that would keep Alicia's mouth shut. His wife, Sherri, began noticing something wrong with the accounts and started asking some questions. So Chris had to be more creative in finding ways of paying Alicia. It wasn't enough, apparently."

"How does this tie into Netstyles?"

"Alicia told Dean that Chris made a promise to her that she would get some profits from this new product that was coming out. She would be set up as a minority private investor in the launch. Dean didn't go into much detail, but to sum it up, what she was going to get from that promise wasn't going to be enough."

"So Chris was planning on giving Alicia some of the profits that were to go to Paul," Jesse deduced. "But how?"

"I'm not sure yet, but whatever it was caught Paul's eye and made him suspicious of it. That's why he hired Sabrina and Tanaka."

"And that's why Chris had them killed," Jesse said. "It's all coming together. You have to call the police, Cole."

"I'm not doing that yet." Cole saw the look of disappointment on her face. "It's not what you think, Jesse."

Jesse shook her head somberly. "It looks like you're riding this for as long as you can, trying to avoid the truth the best you can."

"Jesse, I still have some questions. I still have some doubts." Cole honestly did, and he had searched himself deeply to make sure that was true. "You don't believe me, do you?"

"It doesn't matter." Jesse's hands fell from his shoulders to her sides. "It doesn't matter what I believe. It doesn't matter what is right or wrong. All that matters is that Netstyles and alert.com be saved."

"Jesse, that's not true." Cole reached for her, grabbing

her arm, but she shook free, grabbed her purse from the chair, and headed out. "Jesse, don't leave. I can tell you what my doubts are. You'll understand."

"I don't care," she said, and left the office.

Cole ran after her. He called to her in the hallway near the stairs. "You do care, Jesse. I won't believe that you don't for a second. Don't desert me again."

Jesse swung around to face him. "What do you mean, 'again'?"

Cole had not realized what he had said, but as soon as the words came out, it all hit him. "I need you, Jesse."

"What do you mean, desert you again?" She walked over to him, her head spinning at the thought that his words meant something she understood. Something terribly important.

Cole sat on the bottom step of the stairway in the hall. He waited for Jesse to sit next to him. "You stopped coming."

Jesse knew instantly what he meant, and tears welled in her eyes. He looked at her with a pain in his eyes that reached the deepest parts of her soul.

"I didn't desert you, Cole," she said quietly. "I had to stop . . . stop coming. It was too much to see you every morning."

"But we connected," he said, reliving his feelings from months ago. They were just as fresh today. "We connected and you just stopped coming. I thought it was because of me, something I had done wrong, but I couldn't figure it out. I could tell you didn't want me to approach you, but I thought soon . . ."

"It was me, Cole." Jesse's heart was beating faster than she could ever remember. "I was beginning to care for you. It sounds weird, since we shared no more than a smile and nod to anyone looking."

"But it was more than that," he said, seeking her confirmation.

"Yes, it was," she answered. "It was much more than that, and I was falling for you. The fear that I felt because of Henry hardened my heart and scared it away from you. I had to stop coming, because I knew if we kept it up, eventually we would have to do something about it. I wasn't ready for that."

"Neither of us were," Cole said. "I was caught up with alert.com and with Tracy. I should have never let it go as long as I did with Tracy. But that's over now."

"What do you mean?" Jesse's heart leaped. Was this more of the same? A long distance between two lovers didn't constitute an end to her. Two people were either together or they weren't. And she would never be with a man who was with someone else. No matter how much she wanted him. "What does 'over now' mean?"

Cole found some solace in the fact that she cared. He had made a mess of this with Tracy and she was right to hate him for that alone. "I've been trying to reach her to end it for some time now, but she didn't return my calls. I finally wrote her a letter. I sent it express, so I was able to track it and I know she received it days ago. Tracy is out of my life for good now."

Jesse wasn't sure whether to be happy or scared. Tracy was a barrier between them that, as long as she was there, would keep them apart. With her gone, now what?

"You saw Tracy in my face every day on the beach," Cole continued. "Just like I saw Henry in yours. It was kind of what we communicated to each other in our smiles and nods. But I thought we would be ready one day, and we would keep smiling and nodding until then. I just knew it was going to happen. Then you stopped coming."

"I'm sorry, Cole." She touched his arm. "I did desert you."

"I kept jogging," he said. "I knew you would come back. You had to. Then I saw you across the street from my office that day and I . . . I let this damn product cheat me again. Jesse, I just can't let you go again. I won't."

With tender affection, their faces came together. The heat steamed up their bodies as slowly their cheeks brushed against each other. Jesse let out a whimper as his lips slid by her cheek, barely touching her. His lips tenderly connected with the bridge of her nose. Jesse felt a current of fire speed through her.

Cole's lips sought their sanctuary and claimed it. His desire was nearly punishing. With a force as strong as his emotions, he lifted her into his arms and stood up.

As he carried her up the stairs, Jesse let herself go. She wrapped her arms around his neck. Her head fell back and she let out a moan as his mouth nestled in her neck.

"Oh, Cole," she said, her words barely audible. Passion was coursing through her veins.

Cole groaned as his hands dug into her skin. Her clothes weren't even there to him. At least they wouldn't be for long.

When they reached his bedroom, Cole brought her to the bed. Their eyes connected, and Jesse was ignited by the mischievous smile on his face. She let out a scream as he let her go and she fell to the bed.

When he fell on top of her, he made sure to support himself so as not to hurt her. Playtime was over. His lips came crushing down on hers, and Cole kissed her possessively. His hands caressed her hips with a greed that he was not used to expressing so easily.

Jesse's mind was gone. Her body was a tornado of heat

and urgency. Her tongue explored his mouth, telling him what she wanted. She loved the harsh edge to his lovemaking. She pulled at his T-shirt, her nails trailing along his back.

Cole lifted his arms to let her take his shirt off. He sat up halfway to look down at her. She eyed him seductively, biting her lower lip.

"I've been waiting a long time for this, baby." His hands reached for the bottom of her silk blouse, and he wrapped his fingers around it.

His eyes never left hers as his fingers lifted the top.

"I know we'll make it worth the wait," Jesse said as she let him lift the shirt off of her.

Her hands went to his bare, muscled chest, caressing its hardness. She was filled with a dangerous excitement, knowing where this would go, but letting the road there reveal itself as they went along.

Cole unclipped her bra from the front. Her breasts were not large, but full and as soft as silk. His mouth, his tongue played at them, enjoying the wriggle of her body as it warmed to him.

"Cole!" Jesse felt pleasure radiate through her entire body as his mouth left wickedly wet kisses on her stomach . . . going lower and lower . . .

Control yourself, Cole ordered himself with the last bit of reason he had. He wanted to ravage her, but he would wait. He would wait until he savored every inch of her. Her shorts and panties slid off of her pleasingly curvy hips and down her legs.

Cole pulled her legs to him with gentle ease. He lowered his head to her left thigh, biting it tenderly. He heard her groan as his other hand caressed her right thigh.

She was his.

As Cole leaned over her again, Jesse waited until his lips were only inches from hers before she lifted herself up with all her might. Catching him off guard, Jesse turned swiftly, and in a second she was on top of him.

With a wicked smile, Jesse straddled him. With a sexual aggression she had no familiarity with she grabbed at his khaki slacks and pulled them off. She looked at his body in all its beauty.

He was ready for her. That was undeniable. His eyes told her the same thing. He wasn't used to this, but was liking it. He would let her do whatever she wanted.

He was hers.

"One last thing," she said in a deep, husky voice that was foreign even to her.

Cole nodded to the drawer next to his bed. He stared in amazement at the beauty of her body as she reached inside the drawer for a small foil packet.

He held his hand out to her to accept it, but she shook her head, holding it away. Her eyes teased him as she put it on for him.

"You're wicked," he said, needing to grab at the bed-sheets to keep from grabbing her.

Jesse smiled, rubbing her hands across his flat abdominals. "You have no idea."

When he entered her, all teasing ended. Jesse's eyes closed and the painful pleasure crushed through her.

Cole moaned with desire as his hands gripped her hips. He guided her, although she didn't need it. He was trying hard to keep his eyes open to watch her glorious body, but it was hard. The waves of fire rushing through him were overpowering.

Their bodies created an immediate groove. Their mouths made sounds of ecstasy and heavenly agony. The movements built up speed . . . faster, faster . . . The power of it all brought Jesse down to him. Their lips connected again in frantic desperation.

The noises of passion got louder, their bodies sweating together . . . faster, louder, wetter.

Jesse let out a scream when her body exploded like a volcano. The eruption was complete and soul piercing. She felt her body shiver through and through. A sigh escaped her as every inch of her body tingled.

Cole had been holding it in, but Jesse's explosion was too much for him. When he let it go, his groan reverberated through the room. Those few seconds in a heaven like no other washed over him and set him free.

Exhausted, Jesse fell on top of Cole, her head nestling just under his chin. She couldn't remember ever feeling this way before.

Never before.

Chapter Nine

"With only twenty percent of major Silicon Valley corporations actively involved in recruiting at historically black colleges and universities, there is much work to be done. Other companies say they welcome applicants from these universities, but only pursue minority students at the major universities such as the Ivy League, Big Ten, etcetera. With this philosophy, one fails to see the true commitment."

Jesse looked up from her computer at Joan. "How does that sound?"

Joan's nose crinkled a bit. "Sounds good, but . . . don't you want to end with a zing there? Something that leaves the reader walking away wanting to do something about this?"

Jesse sighed, looking at the words she had just typed on her computer. She was doing this article, this entire series, an injustice. "This topic deserves a better reporter than me."

"How could you say that?" Joan, sitting on the desk next to the computer, gently hit Jesse on the shoulder. "You're a good reporter."

"My head just isn't into this right now," Jesse said. "It's not that I don't care. I really do. I care more about this issue now than when I first started with it."

"Understandable that you would be distracted. You haven't gotten any in a long, long time. That can rattle a gal's brain a little bit."

Jesse laughed, hitting Joan on the knee. "Stop it. I shouldn't have told you about me and Cole."

"I would've killed you if you hadn't, girl. Now admit it, I'm telling the truth."

Jesse leaned back in her chair, a smile coming immediately to her face at the thought of Cole. "I'm in love with him."

"He was that good?"

Jesse's lips curved suggestively. "Actually, yes, he was. But that's not the only reason why. Still, it was different than any other experience I've ever had with a man. It had all the fire and passion that I knew it would, but there was more to it. It was like my body, my heart, had been waiting for that very experience. I felt so . . . so satisfied."

Joan fanned her face with her hand. "Damn, girl."

"Afterward," Jesse continued, "we just held each other. We barely spoke, but it was like we were communicating. One time, I just looked up at him and we both started laughing at the same time. Then he kissed me, and . . . well, we had a long night with hardly any sleep."

"Perfect," Joan said.

Jesse's smile went away. "It was, except for this mess I've

gotten everyone in. I've barely spoken to him in the last few days. Chris has completely lost it with all that's coming out in the news about him.''

"What a freak that guy is. And you say Cole thought he was the best thing since sliced bread?''

Jesse's heart went out to Cole every time she thought of what was coming out about Chris. "He's got to deal with the image he had of Chris falling completely apart at the same time he's doing his job and Chris's job.''

"I know you wish you could be with him.'' Joan reached over and compassionately touched the shoulder she had socked only moments ago. "But you will eventually. These things happen and they have to be taken care of.''

"But this is all my fault,'' Jesse said. "Being with Cole and trying to find out who was behind Sabrina's death did one good thing. It brought me back to myself. I feel like the old Jesse.''

"Spirited, open-minded, and meddlesome,'' Joan said. "That's a very good thing, right?''

"But if it weren't for me being so spirited and meddlesome, we wouldn't be in this situation.'' Jesse noticed the pessimistic look on Joan's face. "I'm serious. It was those documents in my car that led Paul to Tanaka. Cole found out, then Chris. Now this.''

"Paul was going to go to Tanaka with or without you. He was determined to find out who was trying to screw him.''

"But if I hadn't given Paul a copy of those documents, he wouldn't have given them to Tanaka. Then, Cole wouldn't have told Chris, who wouldn't have . . .''

"You don't know that. If Chris had Sabrina killed, he would've had anyone Paul contacted killed. You couldn't control that.''

Jesse shrugged. "I just should have given those documents to Cole. If Chris knew he and Cole had the documents that he was looking for, he wouldn't feel the need to kill Tanaka."

"Those documents were very incriminating, from what you tell me. If Chris thought that Paul was trying to expose his questionable character, maybe he was going to kill Tanaka anyway. And besides, he still murdered Sabrina. That had to come out."

"It's causing Cole a lot of pain," Jesse said, her eyes turning to the phone, wishing he would call.

"And it's all Chris Spall's fault," Joan said definitively. "All of it."

Jesse smiled at her friend, who was always on her side. "Thanks, Joan. I need a friend like you right now."

"You need a friend like me always," Joan jumped off the desk. "Feel better?"

"About that, yeah, but I still have some questions."

Joan moaned as she leaned against the wall.

Jesse ignored her. "It's still not clear how Paul found out. He won't answer any of my phone calls. Cole says he hasn't been in the office because the stress has gotten to him. I know he's spoken with the police. And why did Chris make Sabrina look like a suicide, but not Tanaka?"

"So you have doubts. So does Cole. I'm sure it's even harder for him."

"I know. I've been so angry at him, thinking he didn't care. But when you love someone, it's hard to face reality. Especially when there are a lot of doubts that would be reasonable to anyone."

"Look," Joan said. "You have to trust Cole and the police to handle this from here on. When that happens, you and Cole can deal with whatever you need to deal with to make it work between you. Now, you have a story to finish. I want to see a little more zing in your ending."

"Since when did you become my editor?"

The phone rang just as Joan stuck her tongue out and retreated from the cubicle. Jesse's heart jumped as the caller ID told her it was Cole. She almost fell out of her chair reaching for it.

"Cole!" She was never good at playing aloof. When her heart was in it, she was like an open book. "I'm so glad you called!"

Cole smiled all over at the sound of her wonderful voice. He missed her desperately. He needed so badly to hear her. He wanted even more to touch her.

"How are you, baby?" he asked, a mischievous curve taking over his lips as he thought of their night together, as he had virtually every five minutes since it happened.

"I'm worried," she answered. "You're working too hard."

"I have to." Cole looked at all the papers on his desk. He had been doing his job and Chris's. He was dealing with the press and the police at the same time. He had to keep his head about him. "It's like everything is on the edge here."

"Cole, you can handle it. You can handle anything."

Her faith in him meant more than words could ever describe. He loved this woman, and even though it was all happening at the wrong time, he was thankful to God he had found her. He needed her, especially now.

"What's wrong?" Jesse could sense something in his silence. She felt a connection to this man, and didn't need to see him or hear him to tell something had changed. Again.

Cole sighed, looking at all five lines on his phone blinking. "The press, the police, angry investors. Chris was arrested early this morning."

"They found more evidence," Jesse said. That had to be it. He was the number one suspect, but they didn't have much to go on with only the documents.

"They found the gun that killed Tanaka in the pond near Chris's development. About half a mile from his house. They thought to sweep it on a whim. Also . . ."

Also. Jesse's stomach couldn't get any tighter.

"Also," he continued. "The police interviewed Paul. He told them about Sabrina. They're considering it murder now. They're investigating the drug they had first thought she used on herself. They're going to try to add a second count of murder to Chris."

"I knew Paul would do that eventually. He cared about Sabrina." Jesse thought of Felicia, Sabrina's sister, and wondered if she had been notified of this. She needed to give her a call. "What are they saying about the drug so far?"

"The detectives aren't telling me or Chris's lawyers, who I've been in contact with all along. I've called Dean. He's got a lot of contacts in the SJPD. So far, he thinks it might be traceable to a pharmacy in Burbank. Dean will get more information for me."

"Cole, I'm coming over."

"Not right now, Jesse." Cole saw his assistant coming toward his office. "Don't get me wrong. There's nothing I would want more than to be with you, but I have to work."

"I won't bother you, Cole." Jesse just couldn't stand to be away from him. "I won't get in your way. I just . . ."

Cole wanted to say yes so badly. Even just to see her would be a distraction for him right now, and he couldn't afford that. "Jesse, I promise I'll call you the second I can get away. I will see you before this evening is over. I promise that. I've got to go now. My phone is ringing off the hook."

Jesse tried to hide her disappointment. The last thing she wanted to do was make Cole feel bad. "I have to ask for one thing, Cole."

"I know," he added reluctantly. "As soon as I get off the phone with you, I'll call the bodyguard off."

"I know you mean well, Cole. But I hate it. I really can't stand that guy following me around everywhere. Now that Chris is behind bars, I really don't need him anymore."

"As soon as I'm off the phone."

"Thanks, Cole. I'll still see you tonight, right? You promise?"

"Promise."

"Bye, Cole."

"Bye, sweetheart."

Jesse hesitated before placing the phone back on the receiver. She stared at it for a while, wanting nothing more than to be with him.

"Hey . . . hey, earth to Jesse."

Jesse looked up at Joan, whose head was peeking over the cubicle wall.

"Don't even think about it," Joan said.

"What do you mean?"

"I know you well enough to know that look in your eye. He doesn't want you coming by right now."

"How do you know? Were you on the phone?"

"Please, girl. We're in cubes. I can hear you think. I'm right, aren't I?"

Jesse nodded. "He's busy, but I know he needs me. And it might sound selfish, but I need him."

"Your story, remember?"

"I'll take my laptop to his office." Jesse was already shutting down her computer. "I'll E-mail it to you when it's done and you give it to Luke."

"Jesse."

"I can help him," she insisted. "I know I can."

"I wonder if Mr. Cole Nicholson knows what he's gotten himself into by taking you on. You are definitely not house-broken."

"I'm not that bad," Jesse said. "I know how to be a God-fearing Christian woman and do what my man tells me when he's right."

"And of course, you'll be the one who decides when he's right." Joan squinted as she watched Jesse hurry out of the paper's offices.

"Jesse! Jesse!"

Standing in the downstairs lobby of Netstyles, Jesse searched through the crowds of reporters and nosy visitors for whomever was calling her name.

Paul Brown waved his hands furiously as he approached her. "Jesse, what are you doing here?"

"Paul." Jesse's surprise at seeing him quickly turned to pleasure. With security heightened now that the publicity was so high, there was no way she would get upstairs with the maneuverings that she had used before. In addition, the lobby refused to inform Cole that she was there, as he had instructed them to do with anyone. He wasn't seeing anyone who didn't have an appointment. Except police, and only because with them he didn't have a choice.

Her hands latched on to his arm as he used his badge to reach the elevators. "I came to see Cole. How about you? I heard you were too stressed to come into this madness."

Paul stepped aside to let her in the elevators. He joined her, placing his badge against his floor number to close the doors. "I'm better now. I just came from the police station. I think I put the nail in Chris's coffin. Besides, with him in jail, I'm not in danger."

"So you don't think Cole is out to get you anymore." Jesse was hopeful for this.

Paul nodded, although not convincingly. "I guess not. He's not the murdering type. But I know he knew about what Chris was doing to me."

"I don't think he did, Paul. He was so upset over all this. Trust me." Jesse stepped off the elevator as they reached the Netstyles floor. "I wouldn't lie to you about that."

"I don't care. Chris is the one I want. The police told me that he was being blackmailed by one of his lovers. That's how it all happened. He got a little crazy and desperate. He killed Sabrina to quiet her, and he killed Tanaka to quiet him. It was only a matter of time before he got to me."

"He probably would have, Paul." Jesse waited for his badge to open the door to Netstyles. It was full of people coming and going, as well as visible security. She followed Paul down the hallway. "He just had to make sure he took care of everyone who was made privy to the information. Once he got his hands on those documents, you would have been gone."

"Thank God he didn't." Paul exhaled loudly. "I've got to say, I'm still a little worried about the lawyers. Chris has got the best."

"As soon as the police tie him to the drug that killed Sabrina, even Johnnie Cochran couldn't get him off."

They stopped outside of Paul's office. He looked at her.

"Do you think they can? Do you think they would even bother? I kind of got the feeling that Sabrina was icing on the cake for them. They seem more interested in Tanaka, now that they have the gun and a strong motive. That's where they could really win this."

"They'll definitely go for the murder they have the most evidence on," Jesse said, "but if they can trace the drug to him, it's all the better. I know you would want that for Sabrina."

He smiled somberly. "Yes, I would. Poor girl. I just wonder if Chris was stupid enough to let them trace the drug to him."

Jesse hesitated, wondering if she should tell him. He did care about Sabrina. "Can you keep a secret?"

He nodded, leaning in.

"They might have already traced the drug to a pharmacy in Burbank."

His eyes widened. "Really? Wow, that's great news. How do you know?"

Jesse didn't want Paul running to Cole. "I can't tell you exactly, but it's a contact I have through the police department."

"What are you up to?" Paul eyed her suspiciously. "Does Cole know you're doing all of this to bring down his idol?"

"He's not his idol," Jesse said. "Not anymore. I can't tell you more than that."

"You've told me enough." He briefly touched her shoulder. "Brains, beauty, and determination. You deserve better than Cole."

"What do you mean?"

He paused, looking down both ends of the hallway. "If you're being honest with me, you deserve the same. I called Debra, Chris's secretary, to find out what was going on.

Amid all the other drama here, she said that Cole's girl-friend, Tracy, showed up yesterday and she's been hanging around here ever since."

Jesse swallowed hard, her eyes giving her hurt and amazement away immediately. Tracy was here? Cole had let her come by for a visit; he had let her stay. When he'd told Jesse she couldn't? She tried to calm down before jumping to conclusions.

"Thanks, Paul," she said. "I can handle this."

Jesse held her hand to her stomach as she headed for Cole's office. She didn't hear Paul say good-bye or anything else. The doubts fought their way into her mind. They hadn't discussed Tracy since Cole had told her he'd sent the letter and Tracy was out of his life for good. She should have waited until that was confirmed. But how could she? Her heart was driving her with Cole, not her mind.

She heard a woman's voice just outside Cole's open office and positioned herself next to the slim window, hiding behind the wooden door. She felt guilty for spying on them, but she was hoping to prove her doubtful heart wrong before storming in on the two of them.

She peeked inside and saw clearly a woman of unquestionable beauty sitting in the chair on the other side of Cole's desk. Her long legs were crossed, her dress, a sharp peach, was very short and professional. She was thin, her arms long and bedecked with jewelry. Her features were small, but her eyes stood out. They were blue, contrasting her café-au-lait skin tone. Her hair was long and fiery auburn.

Jesse noticed that Cole appeared angry and frustrated. But he wasn't kicking her out.

"Tracy," he said with a heavy sigh. He had to get rid of

her. He thought she had left twice already. "I really have to get back to work."

"We have to talk. You can't get rid of me. I don't care how busy you are."

"How did you get up here, anyway?" he asked. "Security is so tight, it was hard for *me* to get up here."

"You made the mistake of hiring all men for your security. A beautiful face works just as good as any badge. If you use it right."

Cole knew Tracy was never too principled to use her looks to get something she wanted. "Like I said, I really have to work."

"I know." She flipped strands of hair back with long hands and perfectly manicured fingernails. "But you've been working since I got here. That's what your letter was all about. You wrote it to get me here, after all. You were asking me to come back home, back to you."

Back to you? Jesse bit her lower lip. Not possible.

"That was not what that letter was about and you know it." Cole was barely listening to her, but he thought that she sounded crazy.

"Your words said you were breaking up with me, but I read between the lines. You were ending it because it was too hard to be away from me." Tracy smiled a glossy smile. "That's what you wanted to say."

"No, Tracy." He placed his hands on the piles of papers on his desk. He looked at his desk clock. He had a meeting with the advertising department in less than fifteen minutes. "You're pretty good at twisting things to fit your interest, but you stretched pretty far this time. That letter clearly ended things between us."

Jesse felt her body release a little from its tense state. Only a little.

Tracy pressed her lips together tightly. "Whatever the paper said, it's a piece of paper. I'm here in the flesh, and back in the Valley for good. Now, you'll certainly have to reconsider."

Jesse's stomach tightened again.

Cole wouldn't even consider it. "Come on, Tracy. Everything about our relationship was a charade."

"It seems like it may have become that, but it wasn't before I left. And for a while after." She leaned forward in a fluid, effortless movement. There was no harshness to her actions. "Before I left so unwisely, we were having such a time. Dinners in San Francisco, sailing off the bay with Dean and Tanya. How many times did we spend a weekend at the ski resort up north with Chris and Sherri? Those were incredibly romantic weekends. The four of us would spend the day acting like rich fools. Then the two of us would spend the night acting even more foolish. The sex was incredible."

Jesse felt like she was going to be sick.

"We had fun, Tracy," Cole said with a nod and a smile. "I don't regret any of that. Before I dug myself into alert.com and you went off to New York, we were a super couple."

"We can have that back, Cole." She leaned back smoothly, eyeing him seductively. "We can have the dinners, the sailboat rides, the weekends up north. Remember the private beach we spent a couple of days on at . . ."

The beach. That got Cole's attention. The beach made him think of Jesse. "I'm with another woman now, Tracy. That's what I've been trying to tell you. It wasn't anything that I planned. It was . . . you know I wouldn't hurt you on purpose."

"I've heard about her." She smiled at Cole's guilty

expression. "Yes, I called my spies as well before showing up. Jessica Grant. You can't be serious about her. Cole, she's a little hippie. A dirt-poor reporter. Come on."

Jesse gritted her teeth.

"That's enough, Tracy." Cole's tone was dangerous.

"Just look at it," she insisted. "You're a tech addict. You're just as caught up in this e-revolution as I am. She probably doesn't even own a computer. You need someone like me in your life. Someone who would understand that you had to work instead of be home for dinner with mother. Someone who would expect you to do whatever you have to do to get that product out. This Jessica woman isn't that person. She would expect you to put her first, to leave work behind at five-oh-five PM. So you can be home for dinner. She would question the moral incentive behind everything you did. She would make you feel guilty for being who you are."

"You're way off base, Tracy. Jesse is proud of me and what I do."

"If that's so, then why is she trying to ruin it all? Yes, I know about what she's doing to Chris. She's behind all of this, according to Tanya. Dean has been telling her what's going on, and she told me. This . . . Jesse, is what you call her? Cute, very feminine. This Jesse is putting Netstyles in jeopardy."

Jesse felt her entire body tighten.

Cole tried to control his anger and spoke calmly. "You're right, Tracy. Jesse's investigation has put Netstyles in jeopardy."

Jesse felt everything around her stop at his words. She was horrified. She couldn't stand there and listen to this anymore. He did blame her! This couldn't be happening. With her heart splitting into one hundred pieces, Jesse ran away from Cole's office and out of the building as fast as she could.

Cole hesitated, as he thought he heard something outside his office. Standing up from his desk, he walked over to see if anyone was there.

"What's your problem?" Tracy asked.

"I have to make sure a reporter or a cop didn't find their way up here. They're trying to get in here every way they can." He returned to his seat. "Like I was saying, maybe Jesse's investigation has spurred all this on, but she would never, never try to sabotage me or my happiness. She did what was right, trying to find out who murdered a friend of hers. What is happening now is all because of Chris and his reckless, selfish behavior."

"Listen to me, Cole . . ."

"No, Tracy." He leaned against the desk, looking down at her in the chair. "The months you and I spent together were good, they were fun. I respect you and wish you well. But let's face it. I'm not dumping you. This has been over for a long time. We had some good months, but all of those months can't compare to the weeks I've had with Jesse. She's the woman I love and I will be with her. She will support me in my work, even when it means I can't be home for dinner sometimes. And yes, she will expect me to put her first, because I should. And she should question the morality behind the business decisions I make, because I should, too."

Tracy was visibly annoyed yet speechless. Cole felt his point had been made as he returned to his seat.

"She's not a CEO's wife," she said with finality.

"Is that what this is about?" Cole's laugh was laced with disgust. "It is, isn't it? You've come back because, with all that is happening with Chris, you know my move to take over Netstyles is probably going to happen sooner than expected. You want to make sure you're the lady-in-waiting once I'm head honcho."

Tracy appeared unnerved by his words. "Face it. I'm the perfect wife for you, Cole. It's not like I'm a gold digger. I have my own money. It's not like this is an arranged marriage of any kind. We have cared for each other before. And we can again."

"No, we can't." Cole's eyes slanted at her, his mouth tightening, thinning. "After the things you've said about Jesse, I'm happy to say whatever we had is over. I could lose everything or I could be a multimillionaire CEO. Either way, Jesse would love me just the same. You, well, I doubt you would even bother to spit on me if Netstyles went down the drain. You can leave now."

After a long stare, Tracy stood up and left his office. He knew her pride was a little bruised, but her heart was just fine. She would find another millionaire. He'd known she was good at that before he'd started dating her. Part of him was grateful for her display, making it easier for him to end it. She made him more certain about Jesse, too. He needed to be with her, the woman he loved. He had been so stupid to think she would be a distraction.

Well, he thought with a smile, she would definitely be a distraction. There was no getting around that, as attracted as he was to her. But it was a needed distraction.

Just as Cole reached for the phone, Alice Simms popped her head in the office.

"Got a minute?" she asked. "Stupid question, huh?"

He smiled at her, leaning back in his chair. "For both of us. What's up?"

She walked into the office, placing a few sheets of paper

on the desk. "These are the two press releases I want to put out on the wire."

"How did you handle our . . . situation?" He grabbed the sheets and started reading.

"Carefully," she answered. "But I think the time for that is running out. Can you look them over real quick?"

"Cole."

He looked up to see Debra standing in the doorway. She looked at her watch.

"Damn!" He looked apologetically at Janice. "I have a meeting with advertising. I'll have to read these afterward."

"I need to get them to press by two, Cole. I can't send them out without your approval. When I did that two days ago, you reamed me for an hour."

"I'm sorry, Janice. I didn't mean to do that." He stood up, handing the papers to her. "Send them out. I trust you. I promise not to yell."

"I'll hold you to that."

Cole looked back at the phone, thinking of Jesse. He wanted to be with her now, but it wasn't in the cards. He would call her right after the meeting. He couldn't wait to see her again.

Chapter Ten

The advertising meeting ran almost an hour and a half. Most of it was spent with Cole reassuring his team that things would be all right eventually. He could appreciate how important that was, no matter how much of his time it took. He needed his people now more than ever, and they needed to see confidence. Netstyles employed over fifty people, and all of them knew where Cole stood in the line of power. With Chris all but gone now, it was all up to him. And he was up to the challenge. He never even had a chance to doubt that.

Cole grabbed the phone and dialed Jesse's work number before sitting down. He had come into work the very next morning after they'd made love and placed her home and work number on the first two memory dials of his work and cell phones. No sense in delaying that. He would be calling her more than anyone else in his life from that moment on.

"Silicon Valley Weekly. Joan Griffin here."

"Hello, Joan, it's Cole. I'm looking for Jesse."

He heard a sigh on the other end of the phone and a short silence. "She's not here."

"Do you know where she is?" Cole knew something was up.

"I can take a message for you, Cole."

"She'll want to talk to me, Joan. She's been trying to get in touch with me all day. Is she in the ladies' room? I can call back in a few . . ."

"You won't be able to reach her, Cole." There was a definite tone of annoyance in her voice.

"What's going on, Joan?" Cole didn't have the patience for games. "I need to talk to Jesse now."

Another pause. "Cole, I don't know what to tell you, but I doubt she still wants to talk to you as much as she did before."

"Before? What are you talking about?" Cole heard nothing. "Joan, talk to me. I don't have time for this."

"She didn't want me to tell you."

"But you'll tell me anyway, Joan." His tone was direct and authoritative. "Because you know whatever it is, I'll fix it. You don't have to worry about Jesse."

"But I will worry about her, Cole. Because she already feels guilty over everything that has happened and she loves you."

"She told you that?" Cole felt his tired self wake up.

"Yes. She loves you so much that she came over to your offices to be with you even though you asked her not to. She was willing to put all of her responsibilities aside to be a source of support for you."

"She never came by," Cole said, wondering if she'd been turned away at the desk.

"You didn't notice her, but she did come by. She saw you and your girlfriend sharing sweet memories in your office. Tracy, right?"

Had she been the noise he'd thought he'd heard outside his office? "How did she get up here?"

"Does that matter?"

"No, of course not. But it's not like that. Tracy was trying to . . . She misread that whole scene. You have to believe me, Joan. I love Jesse and only Jesse. I wouldn't play her."

"I have a feeling you really mean that. And it wasn't hearing Tracy talk about old times that really upset her, Cole. From what she heard, you agree she's to blame for what's happening right now to Netstyles."

"That's not true at all." Cole felt his heart sink into his stomach. How could he have let this happen? "I have to find her, Joan."

"She didn't even want me to tell you what I have. Cole, she loves you so much that all she could think of was that you didn't need anything extra to worry about."

Cole felt the sting. She cared so much for him that even if he hurt her, she didn't want him concerned about it with all that was going on now. Cole could not believe how lucky he was . . . or could be. "Where is she?"

"I can't help you with that. Really. She just sent me her story a few moments ago via E-mail. So if she isn't home, she's probably off somewhere alone, trying to think."

Alone, Cole thought. He didn't want her alone. "Joan, if you hear from her, you have to tell her to call me. Tell her I can explain everything, that I love her to no end, and I would never ever blame her for any of this."

Cole hung up and immediately dialed Jesse's home. No

answer. Just as the machine picked up, Debra beeped his line. She was told to only beep in emergencies, so he picked up.

"Dean James is here for you."

"Send him in." Cole put the phone down. He needed to focus on the message he would leave for Jesse. He had to make sure he erased her doubts. He would deal with Dean first.

"You're not looking good at all." Dean eyed him with concern as he entered the office. He walked toward the window behind Cole's desk and leaned against it.

"I've upset Jesse." Cole swung around in his chair. "That's the last thing I wanted to do."

"You've got it bad for this woman, don't you?" There was a tiny smile on Dean's face.

"More than bad," Cole said, wringing his hands together. "She's it for me, Dean. I want to be with her forever."

"You mean you've actually found a woman you would rather spend more time with than this desk?"

Cole laughed. "Now, that's not fair. I'm not a complete work hound."

"You have been lately."

"Well, regardless. I have finally found her, and the thought of hurting her upsets me more than any of this mess that's going on." He waved his hand over his desk.

"Well, I've got good news and bad news for you. What do you want first?"

"Good," Cole answered. "I need some."

"The good news is that you're in love."

"Quit kidding around, Dean. What are you here for?"

Dean laughed. "Obviously your sense of humor is gone. Okay, my source says the cops have traced the drug to a pharmacy on Allen Street in North Burbank. It's a small but very active pharmacy because it carries a lot of health crap, and it's located underneath a big Gen-X health-club-slash-meat-market."

"Can they trace it back to Chris yet?" Cole had to accept the inevitable. Chris was probably going to jail. He no longer held on to hope about that.

"Not yet. You know Chris lives in the Santa Clara Hills, so there would be no reason for him to go to this club or pharmacy. Which is the whole point, right? The cops are supposed to be checking prescriptions and credit card receipts, but they've got to go back a ways. The medical examiner says he knows how old the drug is, but that was within a month or two range. They're working on it."

"What's the bad news?"

"Chris is out on bail."

Cole was surprised. "What are you talking about?"

"Those damn lawyers you rich guys have can work wonders. Man, I wish I could have afforded one when I was caught hacking. But yeah, he's out. He's out on some insane amount of bail. The judge placed it high, the normal amount for murder. But the state must not have made it clear to him what means the defendant had."

Cole didn't doubt that Chris had the cash for the ten percent needed to bail himself out. He might have even put his house up, which Cole knew was worth at least three million dollars. He'd never expected the judge to allow bail.

"Even with the gun?" he asked.

"His fingerprints aren't on it. And it was found outside his development. The defense will have a field day with that."

"Damn," Cole said as his phone rang. He noticed the number on the caller ID. "It's Chris's cell phone."

He looked at Dean for a moment before picking up. "Chris?"

"How could you let this happen to me, Cole?" His voice sounded erratic and panicked. "How could you let that bitch do this to me?"

"Don't you ever, ever call Jesse that," Cole said. "Now, calm down. Where are you?"

"Her and Paul. They're in this together. They're trying to destroy me. They already have. It didn't have to become this, Cole. If you had stuck by me, it wouldn't have gotten to this."

"Chris, I have done more for you than anyone, but the evidence is overwhelming."

"I knew you would join them! Is she that good, Cole? She sure whipped you around quick. Fine, that's fine. That's all fine. Sherri left me. I don't even know where she took the kids. Everyone has deserted me, the press has destroyed me. If I'm going to be accused, tried, and convicted of murder, I might as well get something out of it."

"Chris!" Cole knew exactly what he meant by that. "Chris! Chris! Chris!"

The line was dead. Cole called Chris's cell phone back, but couldn't even get a dial tone. He slammed the phone down.

"What?" Dean's face reacted to the extreme alarm on Cole's.

Cole shot up from his desk. "He's angry. He's given up. He's going after Jesse, and I think Paul, too."

"What do you want me to do?" Dean followed Cole, who was out of his office and at the elevator in moments. "You called the bodyguard off of her, didn't you?"

"As soon as I found out that Chris was in jail. Okay, Dean, I need you to call the police first." He was trying to talk as fast as he was thinking. "Have them get over to Jesse's right away. Tell them Chris threatened to kill her. Then, head down the hall and tell Paul. He needs to get one of the security guards in this building to stay right on him. I'm going to get Jesse. I'll meet the police there."

Dean took out a pad and pencil. "Address?"

Cole gave him the information just before the elevator closed in front of him. He had to find Jesse in time. He would die if anything every happened to her. Especially if it was because of him. After all of this, he couldn't possibly lose her. She was his future, his life. . . .

He dialed her home number on his cell phone. No answer again. He waited impatiently for the machine to pick up.

He made sure to keep his voice calm. "Jesse, first of all, about Tracy, please don't be upset about that. I handled her and she's out of our lives forever. I love you and nothing else matters more than that. No matter what you heard, I don't blame you for anything. I need to thank you for doing what was right when I wasn't sure if I could. Most important, you have to call me right away. Chris is out of jail and he's lost his mind. He's after you and Paul and he's dangerous. He doesn't care what happens to him now that he's lost everything. Dean called the police, and I'm coming over right now."

The late afternoon jog had done Jesse good. Instead of eating an entire pizza as she had wanted to do when Joan forced her to go home from work because she was so upset over Tracy, Jesse'd thrown on her workout gear and cranked the Walkman up. She had been jogging for almost an hour and now that she was back at her house, she felt one hundred times better than when she'd first stepped off her stairs. Her endorphins had kicked in.

She had had enough of these doubts, these uncertainties. The old Jesse was never such a wimp. She wasn't giving up, she wasn't losing out. Whatever it was that Tracy wanted from Cole wasn't important. Jesse loved him, more than she had ever loved any man, and she was going to hold on to him. She was going to hold on to him and make him understand why she did what she did. She would see to it that he understood. She didn't doubt that he would. He would love her.

Her fear, Henry, and all the other relationship mistakes she had made in the past had just piled on the scene she had witnessed between Tracy and Cole. But she wasn't giving in to that anymore. Henry was out of her life and she had to let that go. She couldn't change the person she was and be happy at the same time. The person she was—would always be—jumped into love. She couldn't help it. She was a feeling person, a heart-first-mind-later type of sister.

And, as she stepped inside her house, leaving the door open, only the screen door closed, Jesse had a feeling that with Cole, she would never regret being the kind of person she was. That was how she knew he was the man for her. She would not have to think about why she loved him or if she should love him. She just did, very much, and everything was okay.

She had left the door open because she intended to get some writing done on the front porch since it was such a nice day. But, first things first, she went for the phone. She had to call him to hear his voice, to reassure herself and let him know how much she loved him. She wouldn't bother him about Tracy right now. He didn't need the extra worry. It would be resolved, but not now. Now, she wanted to . . .

Noticing the answering machine blinking, she pressed the Play button. When Jesse heard Cole's voice, her entire body quivered in pleasure.

"Jesse, first of all, about Tracy, please don't be upset about that. I handled her and she's out of our lives forever. I love you and nothing else matters more than that. No matter what you heard, I don't blame you for anything. I need to thank you for doing what was right when I wasn't sure if I could."

Jesse's smile was ear to ear. She could hug the answering machine right now. Her hand picked up the phone headset, but she froze in place as she listened to the rest of the message.

"Most important, you have to call me right away. Chris is out of jail and he's lost his mind. He's after you and Paul and he's dangerous. He doesn't care what happens to him now that he's lost everything. Dean called the police, and I'm coming over right now."

Jesse gasped, her hand coming to her chest. Chris was out of jail and coming after her! Her eyes searched around quickly, her mind trying to figure out what she needed to do. The door! The screen door wasn't even locked.

Jesse ran to the door. She jumped back with a horrified scream as a large figure stepped right in front of her. On the other side of the screen, a troubled-looking Paul stared at her.

"My God, Paul!" Jesse had to lean against the door to hold herself up. "You scared me to death. Bad choice of words, but you know what I mean."

"What's wrong with you, Jesse?" His left hand pressed against the door. "You're the palest sister I've ever seen. Are you alone here?"

She stepped away from the door. "Get in here and close the door behind you. You're not safe out there."

Paul stepped inside, but didn't close the door as directed. "What's going on?"

Jesse sat on the sofa in her living room, not noticing that the door had not been shut. "Chris got out of jail."

"I know," he said. "My lawyer called me and told me a few minutes ago. I was on my way to the post office. I just kept driving. I didn't know what to do. I realized I was close to your place, so I stopped by. Are you here by yourself?"

"Yes, I am," Jesse answered. "Cole says Chris is after us. He doesn't care about anything. How did you know where I live?"

"I figure Chris is angry enough at me to kill me, but how do you know he's after the two of us?"

"Listen to this." Jesse got up and replayed the message from Cole.

She watched Paul as he listened intently. She watched as his face went from curious to serious, then to a smile . . . *a smile.*

"You think this is funny?" Jesse's hands were on her hips. Looking past him, she realized the door was still open. "You didn't close the . . ."

"I don't think it's funny," he said slowly. "I think it's perfect."

The look on his face alarmed Jesse. He was on the verge of laughing. Had Paul lost it, too?

"You're crazy," she said as she passed him heading for the door. "I have to close this . . ."

Suddenly, Jesse felt Paul grab her by the arm and jerk her back so hard that she fell to the floor. She looked up at him, her eyes and mouth wide open.

"Paul, what are you doing?" She tried to lift herself off the ground, but he stepped over to her, practically standing over her.

"Well, Jesse." He reached in his back pants pocket and pulled out a handgun so small it looked like a toy. "No need to waste time. You should know, I'm going to kill you."

Jesse watched with horror as she realized what was in his hand. But she didn't understand.

"Correction," he said as he reached down and pulled her up harshly. "Chris is going to kill you. At least that's what the police will think when they show up."

Jesse tried to pull free of him and turn away, but he twisted her arm until the pain was excruciating. She let out a scream.

"None of that," he said. "You scream and you're killing Cole, too."

"What do you mean?" she asked, horrified.

"You haven't figured it all out yet? I thought you reporters were supposed to be so smart. I killed Sabrina, Jesse. I killed Tanaka, too."

"But why?" Jesse could barely speak through her shock. "You cared about Sabrina. You said you did."

"I lied," he said as nonchalantly as if he were ordering takeout. "Back to what I was saying. You want to scream? Go ahead. I'll just have to kill Cole as soon as he arrives."

"But the police could arrive first." Jesse was trying hard to think. She knew to stall. *Stall.* Cole would be there soon. The door was wide open.

"Do you want to take that chance?" His eyebrows narrowed, almost jokingly.

"No, I don't, Paul." She looked at the door. "Just let me go lock the door, so no one can get in here."

"Go ahead." He waved the gun at her, giving her permission. "Don't try anything."

Jesse's target was her purse, left on the table near the front door as usual. She had Mace in there. That was all she had. She had to stall. With her back to him, Jesse closed the front door, pretending to lock it to give Paul a sense of security. The door made the same clicking sound if you turned it left or right. Left locked it. Right did nothing. She turned it right.

She turned back to him. He was facing her. The gun in his hand was pointed down, not at her. Jesse saw this as a good sign. He didn't really want to kill her. She had to stall, catch him off guard, and have a chance to get away from him.

"Can I ask for one thing, Paul?" Jesse found a tone of voice within herself that was as sweet as sugar, almost childlike.

"A favor?" he asked, smile gone now. "Do you know how much trouble you've made for me here? Well, I guess this message here makes up for it."

He reached over and clicked the Save button, making the message light flash again. "So, fine. What can I help you with?"

"Tell me why." Jesse genuinely wanted to know. "I don't understand why you would do this. It seemed so clear that Chris did . . ."

"Genius, isn't it?" he said, interrupting her. "I guess it's fine. It's not like you're going to tell anyone."

Jesse swallowed hard and cursed him in her mind. She

was not going to die. She was not going to let that happen. She stepped in front of the table. Reaching behind her back the second he turned away to take a seat, she realized her purse was zipped. This would be harder than she thought.

"I'll give you the short version," Paul said. His face appeared very serious, although his voice sounded almost sarcastic. "I kind of always knew that Chris regretted that Cole hired me. You see, Chris was already dealing with Cole, who was twice as smart as he was. Then I came along, and Chris felt threatened. But I'm used to that. Anyway, it's like I told you, they started leaving me out of alert.com meetings. Leaving me off the memos."

"Cole said this was a need-to-know project," Jesse said. "How can you be sure that wasn't all that was? You know how protective people have to be in your industry."

Paul shook his head. "You don't understand. I was completely cut off. Like I was a stranger. So I did a little investigation of my own. You're not the only expert at getting past the Nazi-style security we have at the office. You see, Chris has this problem. It drives Cole crazy and he gets on him all the time. Chris throws everything in the garbage. Whether it's garbage, recyclables, or 'must be shredded.' Cole's pet peeve."

"You went through his garbage and found out about what he was promising Alicia?" With one hand in front of her, Jesse opened the zipper of her purse behind her one stitch at a time. No noticeable movement.

"You missed your calling, Jesse. I should've hired you for a P.I."

"So you could set me up to be murdered, too?"

A smile formed at the edges of Paul's lips for only a second. "I found a draft, an extremely early draft, but a draft of something Chris sent to one of his personal lawyers. In a word, it was funneling some of alert.com's profits to Alicia. The profits would come from a secondary postrevenue account, which is where my shares for helping bring the product to life were to come from. Cole and Chris were sharing from the primary profits. I didn't know who the hell this woman was. I didn't care. It was my money. So, I hired Sabrina to find out what Chris was up to."

"So you lied when you said you . . ."

"No, I met her at the gym and she wouldn't leave me alone. I humored her. When I found out what she did for a living, I hired her to check on Chris and find some documents that I was conveniently left off of. It was amazing what she found out about Chris. I had no idea. He seemed like a pompous jerk, but not a whoremonger like he was. This chick was going to blackmail him for all he was worth to keep quiet about this love child they had together. You see, Chris made all his millions after he married Sherri. So, if they were to get divorced, which, knowing Sherri, would most certainly have happened, she would get half. Good old state of California divorce law. Led many a man to do the unthinkable rather than risk a divorce. This gave me a great idea. I could kill two birds with one stone. Get rid of Chris and keep my money."

"By killing Sabrina?" The purse was open. Jesse tried to keep her expression still. Where was Cole? Where were the police? She could not count on anyone but herself right now.

Paul sighed. "You know this Internet world. Cutthroat doesn't even describe it. No such thing as cutting edge. The word now is *bleeding edge,* and that is no pun. It would make perfect sense if Chris were to kill Sabrina. After all, she was exposing him to be this borderline pervert who was also compromising his business reputation and integrity. He would be ruined. So, she's dead and the police find all the proof they need to lead them to Chris. He's in a jail, and out of my way.''

Jesse was distracted, her concern for Sabrina drawing her attention to him. "You killed Sabrina to frame Chris? Then why did you try to make it look like a suicide?"

Anger framed his face. "You. Because you took the files that she had on Chris!"

"I didn't take them, Paul. She left them in my car by accident.''

"I came by for dinner. She said she couldn't do it anymore. She was tired of spying on people for a living and wanted to get away from it all. So, I had to take care of her. I was going to be merciful. So I drugged her with a mix of prescriptions. I got the information on which ones to mix from the Internet. Then I realized the file was missing. I was going to leave it to make it look like she was trying to hide it from whoever killed her. Without her, I couldn't find the file, but I couldn't risk her coming to and telling the cops that I drugged her. So, I had to give up on her and start again. I forced more of the drug down her and waited until she . . . died. Then I cleaned the place up. I had really messed up.''

Jesse couldn't hide the look of disgust on her face.

"So," Paul went on, "I had to try again to frame Chris. This time I found Tanaka just looking through the yellow pages. I thought I'd have to start all over, but thanks to you giving me the documents, I didn't have to wait long to get rid of him. I gave him all that Sabrina had put together, including a little mock-up of her notes saying that she thought Chris was on to her and she was getting scared. I had to type it, because her writing could not be duplicated. It was all perfect. You were on my side, and that would come in handy in the future.

"With Tanaka dead, I made sure to add a little Post-it, nothing formal, noting in some way he was concerned about Chris as well. I placed it in a way that would make it seem like Tanaka was trying to hide it from someone who was coming to visit him. He had his back to me. He never saw it coming. That was all I needed to frame Chris. He would be out of the way, and Cole wouldn't screw me. He's a shrewd businessman, but he would have felt so sorry for me he would certainly give me more than even before. And with him CEO, I could be chief architect."

"So why me now, Paul?" Jesse had her hand on the Mace. She gripped it tightly. "You had it all going your way. Chris was about to be ruined."

"It's my fault mostly." He bit his lower lip until it started to bleed. "I should've let Sabrina alone. I just got so excited about everything working out that I got carried away. So I told them about Sabrina and what I suspected. So that led everyone on a goose chase to find the drug that killed her. I did a good job of covering my tracks, but you . . . you scared me."

"What did I do?" Jesse needed him to come to her. That way she could mace him and get out the front door in a split second. She could run faster than light if her life depended on it.

"They were going to track the drug to the Nutrition Center. It's underneath the health club that Sabrina and I belonged to. You knew about the club, and it would only be seconds before you would make the connection and cause all kinds of trouble. So I had to do something about you. But what?"

"You'd just figure that out once you got here?" *Come to me,* she said to herself. She would not die today.

"Yes." He stood up, stretching his arms. "But I guess I'm about as lucky as they come. On my way over here, my lawyer tells me that Chris is out of jail. That message from Cole leads you right into Chris's path. He kills you the second he gets out. I'm back at full strength. That is . . . as soon as I take care of you."

Jesse knew this was the last chance she would get. He would not come any closer. Just as she pulled the Mace out of the purse, she heard a gasp escape Paul. She felt herself being pushed aside from the left and turned to the door.

Chris Spall came barreling into Jesse's house with the face of a madman. His blond hair was a disheveled mess, his eyes and nose red as beets. His clothes were a dirty, sweaty mess.

Jesse fell back. She turned to Paul and saw what could only be described as shock on his face. As his hand, holding the gun, began to rise, Chris let out a maniacal yell and raised his own hand. The reflection of the shiny silver pistol set off a glare that blinded Jesse. She heard a gunshot and then silence. When she could see again, Paul was on the floor, and blood was on his shirt. He was holding his lower stomach and coughing.

"Oh my God!" Jesse backed up farther as Chris turned to her. She saw what was in his eyes. He cared for nothing, and that was worse than hate.

"You two," he said, his voice as ragged as his appearance. "You two destroyed my life. I can't go back now. I have nothing. I had everything and now I have nothing."

"That's not true," Jesse said. "Everyone will know that. Paul did all of this. You'll be freed and cleared. I promise.

If we can go to the police, this will all be erased and you'll have it all back. . . ."

Chris seemed to pause for a second. "He . . . what could . . . to hell with it all, anyway. I just killed him. I'm going down. And besides, nothing can bring back my wife, my reputation. No one in this industry will want to do business with me again. They'll never believe I'm not holding back the profits from them. You and Paul are to blame for all of this."

"So you're going to kill us and go down for four murders?" Jesse pointed to Paul. "You'll get the death penalty for sure. Look at Paul. He's still alive. If we can get him to a doctor in time, you won't have killed anyone. You can save your life here. You can . . ."

She stopped as she heard the click of the hammer and saw the gun pointed at her. Chris was almost shaking. He seemed to be holding his breath. Jesse knew now was the moment of truth.

"What about Cole?" she yelled out.

She saw him blink, then begin to breathe again. Slowly the gun lowered. She heard the click of it being uncocked.

"Cole loves me," she continued. "And he loves you, too. What would this do to him? It will destroy him."

"He's turned on me." Chris's arms fell limp at his sides.

"Cole never turned on you. He had no choice but to believe what all the facts were saying. Even still, this morning he called me and was so upset to hear you were arrested. He still cares for you so much."

Chris nodded as he turned away. "You can't begin to understand me and what I do. Why I do. What this all means to me."

"Netstyles means everything to Cole. You know that. You shared that love." Jesse felt herself calming down. She had reached him. Now, all she needed was time. She heard a car door slam. She felt herself exhale.

"For Cole," he said with a sigh. "For Cole, I won't kill you. I owe him that much."

Chris backed up against the wall and slid down to the floor, where he curled up in a fetal position. He started weeping, and Jesse felt almost compelled to go to him.

"Jesse!" Cole burst through the door and came face-to-face with Chris, the gun by his side.

"Cole!" Jesse ran to him and jumped into his arms. She began crying as he kissed her face repeatedly. "Thank God, Cole. I thought it was all over."

"I'm here, Jesse." He heard the sirens in the background. He saw Paul on the ground, moaning in pain. "I'm here."

Epilogue

Jesse sipped her glass of wine as she watched Cole surrounded by well-wishers. Tonight was his night, and she had never been so proud. Tonight at the annual Silicon Valley Technology Awards dinner, the coveted prize for best consumer product of the year had gone to alert.com and Netstyles. The look on Cole's face as he'd accepted the award as CEO had been so full of joy and pride that Jesse had cried . . . especially when he'd thanked her.

Now she watched as he tried to make his way to her. He had been trying all night, looking incredible in his tailored tux. But every step he took, he was stopped not only by well-wishers, but also by businessmen wanting to get a piece of the pie, professionals wanting to work for him, and media hounds wanting to put his picture on the cover of every technology and marketing magazine in the country.

This was the good part. But it had taken a voyage through a lot of bad to get to this October evening. Five months cleaning up the mess that Chris and Paul had made.

Chris Spall was charged with the attempted murder of Paul Brown, but with five-hundred-dollar-an-hour lawyers, his plea of temporary insanity came through for him. He was in a country club type mental hospital, his chances of getting out within a year very good.

Attempted murder charges were based on the fact that Paul did not die. After recovering from his wounds, Paul was charged with two counts of first-degree murder of Sabrina and Tanaka and one count of attempted murder of Jesse. The trial was swift due to the publicity, and Paul was sentenced to life in prison, without possibility of parole.

Cole was made CEO of Netstyles and released alert.com in June, with the help of a newly hired Hispanic chief architect and a promoted African American director of business development. The product exploded onto the market, and Cole became a millionaire many times over. The fact that an almost completely minority-run company had left all others in the dust didn't hurt the publicity either.

Most of all, Jesse thought as her heart warmed, she and Cole had been together through all of it. A source of comfort for each other, their love had grown quickly. Every moment they could, which wasn't often due to Cole's sudden fame, they would make love and talk each other's ears off. They began jogging together on the beach every day, laughing and falling into each other's arms every time they passed the bench that marked their first few meetings. The meetings where their hearts grew to know each other—to love each other—before they had spoken a word.

"Finally." Cole reached Jesse, delighted beyond words

to finally connect with her. The night had been overwhelming for him, almost like a drug. "I lost you."

Jesse's lips met his in a tender kiss that still managed to get her pulse racing. He could do that with nothing. "Thought I'd give you more time in the sun. You're the man of the day. After all, it's what you did for me last month when I won my award."

"Journalist of the year from the California chapter of the NAACP." He remembered the proud moment. "You're really something."

"Stop it," she said, allowing him to wrap his arms around her and pull her to him. "That was nothing compared to this."

"I wouldn't say that. Your series has breathed some new life into the fight to get more minorities in positions of power in this area and tech centers all over the country. That's a big deal."

"Stop trying to avert the glory. Tonight is about you, baby." Jesse ran her finger down his left cheek. She loved him for sharing her pride in her own work.

"What could be more perfect than tonight?" He loved her so much, he never wanted to let her go. Being away from her for even a day had become unbearable at times. "Let's go away for the weekend. Let's do something special."

Jesse sighed. "I can't. Honey, I've been so caught up in work and you, that I haven't been looking for a place to live. It's October and the family I'm renting from is coming back in fifteen days. I've got to find a place I can move into in the next couple of weeks."

"What about moving in with me?" He had planned on asking her to move in this weekend, although he should have done it earlier. No time better than the present.

Jesse's eyes widened. She searched her feelings. She felt disappointed. Shouldn't she be happy? "You want us to live together?"

"Well . . . yes, I . . ." Something was wrong. She was upset. He could read her emotions very easily. She never tried to hide them, and he loved that about her. Among other things. "You don't want to live together, Jesse?"

Jesse shrugged. She had hoped for more. "Well, I guess. I don't know. I thought . . ."

"Jesse, can I be honest with you?" He placed the award on the table against the wall of the ballroom. "I don't want us to live together."

Jesse felt a jab to her stomach. He didn't even want to live with her. "Why did you offer it? Because you felt sorry for me?"

"No, fool. I asked you because you're such a free spirit, Jesse. You're extremely independent. Don't get me wrong, I love that about you. I figure something as traditional as marriage wouldn't interest you."

"No, it . . ." Jesse heard herself almost yelling she was so excited. She calmed herself down. "No, it does. I mean, yeah, I'm a modern woman. But marriage isn't old-fashioned, not to me at least. I think in this day and age, marriage is actually quite a break from the norm, which you know I like."

Cole smiled. "Well, then. I don't want you to move in with me, Jesse Grant. I want you to marry me."

Jesse wrapped her arms around him and kissed him hard. "Of course I will. I can't wait to marry you, Cole."

"You realize you've made this night so perfect I can barely stand it." He leaned against the wall. "I think I might have to sit down I'm so happy. You're making me the happiest man in the universe."

Jesse was filled with love for this man with whom she was going to spend the rest of her life. "Oh, one more thing."

"What else?" he asked. "I don't think I can take any more happy news."

"I know you said you don't want me to move in with you."

"Not at all." He waved his hand. "Marriage or nothing, woman. That's my final offer."

"Well, I need a place to stay." She batted her eyelashes at him. "So can we speed this marriage thing up a bit?"

He placed his forehead against hers and whispered, "We can be in Vegas in two hours. Why don't you make an honest man out of me tonight?"

"If you need it that bad."

Their lips connected again and never let go.

ABOUT THE AUTHOR

Angela Winters was born and raised in a suburb of Chicago. She is the youngest of six children. After graduating from high school, she majored in journalism at the University of Illinois at Urbana-Champaign and worked as a beat reporter for the *Daily Ilini*. She graduated in 1993, and worked in financial public relations, marketing, and executive research. She is currently a consultant for a northern Virginia financial services company.

Angela is currently a member of Romance Writers of America, Mystery Writers of America, Sisters in Crime, and Washington Romance writers.

E-mail her at angela-winters@yahoo.com

Or visit her Web site:
  http://www.tlt.com/authors/awinters.htm